Cara Colter shares her life in beautiful British Columbia, Canada, with her husband, nin̶ horses and one small Pomeranian with a large attitude. She loves to hear from readers, and yo̶ can learn more about her and contact her throug̶ Facebook.

KV-197-073

HIS CONVENIENT ROYAL BRIDE

CARA COLTER

MILLS & BOON

Published in Great Britain 2019
by Mills & Boon, an imprint of HarperCollins*Publishers*
1 London Bridge Street, London, SE1 9GF

© 2019 Cara Colter

ISBN: 978-0-263-07986-9

MIX
Paper from
responsible sources
FSC
www.fsc.org   FSC˚ C007454

Printed and bound in Great Britain
by CPI Group (UK) Ltd, Croydon, CR0 4YY

To all my brave friends entering civic politics—Bill, Debbie, Ellen, Karen—intent on changing the world for the better in their own way, with their own gifts.

CHAPTER ONE

"LOOK, MADDIE, IT'S THEM."

"Sorry, who?" Maddie asked, distracted. The Black Kettle Café opened for the day in—her eyes flew to the clock—thirty minutes.

She checked inventory. The glass-encased shelves were lined with an abundance of scones, in six different flavors. The scones were her idea. She felt her stomach knot with familiar anxiety. What if it was too early to put out so many? Should she have waited for the weekend concert crowds? What if she had spent all that money on something that wouldn't sell? Wouldn't it have been better to chip away at some of the overdue bills?

And then there was the ever-present voice of self-doubt. *What kind of an idiot thought scones could save a business?* And deeper yet, *Was there any point in saving a business in a town that was probably going to die, despite her best efforts?*

"Those awesomely attractive men I told you about. A perfect ten on the ooh-la-la scale. Both of them. Don't you think that's unusual? Two perfect tens together?"

Maddie bit her lip in exasperation. The weight of the whole world felt as if it was resting on her not-big-enough shoulders, and her young helper was rating every male she saw on an ooh-la-la scale? Sophie probably wouldn't be nearly as excited about the awesome attractiveness of the visitors, if she knew Maddie was worried about how the café was going to pay her wages!

It was Sophie's first day working the coffee shop in the remote town of Mountain Bend, Oregon. Sophie, just out of high school, was the summer help and she was easily distracted and resisted direction. She had not wanted to put on an apron this morning, because it "hid her outfit."

Though technically Maddie was the café manager, there were several problems with reprimanding her. Sophie was the owner's niece. And she and Maddie had grown up practically next door to each other in the small village. Maddie felt almost as if they were sisters—older and younger.

"What men?" Maddie asked reluctantly.

"I told you! I saw them last night. They're driving the sports car. A Lambo in Mountain Bend. Can you believe it?"

Maddie had no idea what a Lambo was and, unless it was fueled by scones, she didn't really care.

"They're jaw-dropping," Sophie decided dreamily. "I like the big one. He's got a certain formidable look about him, doesn't he? Like he might be a cop. He wasn't driving, though. The other one was driving. They're right outside the door. For heaven's sake, quit scowling at me and look!"

Against her better judgment, Maddie followed Sophie's gaze out the large, plate glass window. The quaint main street—and all her troubles—faded into nothing. Maddie was not aware of the loveliness of overflowing flower baskets, or that the stone-fronted buildings were, like the house she had inherited, showing signs of disrepair.

Maddie was aware, suddenly and intensely, of only *him*. Some energy, some power, shivered around him, and it dimmed even the extraordinary morning light that lit the lush green forest that carpeted the steep hills that embraced Mountain Bend.

The day's menu was posted, and two men were studying it. It was true, the bigger of them was memorable—large, muscled, redheaded, with a thick beard that matched his hair. The man was definitely a throwback to some kind of Gaelic warrior.

But regardless of his obvious power, he was not the one who had made the entire world fade into nothingness for Maddie.

It was the man who was with him. A full head shorter than his companion—which still would have made him just a hair under six feet tall—the other man radiated power and presence, a kind of rare self-confidence that said this man owned the earth and he knew it.

Tall and well built, he was stunningly gorgeous. His thick, neatly trimmed hair was as rich and chocolaty as devil's food cake. He had high cheekbones, a straight nose, a chin with a faint—and delicious—hint of a cleft in it. He glanced away from the menu, through the window and straight at Maddie.

Her thought was to duck, as if when he saw her, he would know there was something weak melting within her, like an ice-cream cone that had toppled onto hot pavement. But she found herself unable to move, in the grip of a dark enchantment. All her sensations intensified as his gaze met hers. His eyes were deep blue, ocean water shot through with sapphires. A hint of pure fire sparked in their endless depths.

She was shocked by the reappearance of a demon within her. But there it was: pure, undiluted, primal attraction to a gorgeous man. Good grief! How many times did a woman have to learn life's most unpleasant lessons?

There was no one riding in to the rescue.

Though maybe this was the sad truth: in times of stress, there was no drug more potent than an extraordinarily attractive man, the fantasy that someone would come along and provide respite from the onerous challenges of daily life.

And since there was no arguing the stressfulness of

these times—Past Due notices stacking up like a deck of cards in the café office—Maddie indulged the feeling of unexpected magic whispering into her life.

Her eyes dropped to the full, sinfully sensual curl of a firm bottom lip, and she felt the most delightful shiver of, well, longing. To be transported to the place that a kiss from lips like those could take you.

That was not real. A place of weakness, she reminded herself, annoyed by her lapse. Fairy tales did not exist. She had found that out the hard way. Maddie gave herself a determined mental shake. It was the strain of her life that was making this small diversion seem so all encompassing.

If this was a test, she was as ready for it now as she would ever be.

"Go let them in," she said to Sophie.

Sophie gave her a startled look—they never opened early—and then dashed for the door, divesting herself of that hated apron on the way, and pulling the ribbon from her hair. Sophie's romantic schoolgirl notions could be forgiven—she *was* just a schoolgirl—but Maddie was twenty-four.

She had lost both her parents. She had lived and worked in New York City. She had suffered a heartbreaking betrayal from a man she had thought she would marry. She had come home to find the café and her town struggling. Really, all these events—the awareness that life could turn bad on a hair—should be more than enough to make her jaundiced forever.

Despite being jaundiced forever, Maddie found her hand going to her hair, light brown and short, with the faintest regret. She had cut it in the interest of being practical, particularly now that her dreams were all business based, but still it shocked her every time she looked in the mirror. The shorter cut had encouraged waves to tighten into corkscrews. Coupled with her small frame, instead of achieving the practical professional look she had aimed for, Maddie felt she looked as if she was auditioning for the part of a waif in a musical.

"Good morning, gentlemen," Sophie sang as she opened the door.

Maddie felt a hint of envy at Sophie's easy vivaciousness, her delight in the potential for excitement. She could warn her, of course, that the path was fraught with danger and betrayal, but Sophie wouldn't listen. Who believed, in the flush of youthful enthusiasm, such things could happen to them?

Hadn't she known, in her heart, her parents would not have approved of the supersuave Derek? Hadn't people tried to tell Maddie that her fiancé might not be worthy of her? Including the friend who had—

"Welcome to the Black Kettle, the coffee shop that won the People's Choice award for Mountain Bend."

This was news to Maddie, but Sophie had decided she would take marketing when she saved up enough money for college. She obviously was testing her skills and looked pleased with the result.

Because the men, if they had been debating whether to stop in, suddenly had no choice.

"Thank you," the darker, younger one said, moving by Sophie first.

His voice was deep and velvet edged, as confident as everything else about him. In those two words, Maddie detected a delightful accent. Maddie felt the air change in the room as soon as he entered, something electrical and charged coming through the door with him.

Electricity is dangerous, she told herself primly. *Not to mention expensive.*

"Good morning," Sophie said, beaming at his larger

companion and batting her thick lashes at him. The man barely glanced at Sophie.

Instead, he surveyed the coffee shop, tension in his body and the set of his jaw, as if he was scanning for danger.

In a just-opening coffee shop in Mountain Bend?

For a reason, she could not put her finger on, Maddie thought that the men did not quite seem equals, the younger man effortlessly the leader between them.

"We aren't usually open yet," Sophie said to the bigger man's back. "But you looked like a couple of hungry guys."

"Thank you," the other said, his pleasantness making up for his friend's remoteness. "That's very kind. We are hungry. It would be dinnertime where we are from."

That accent, Maddie decided, could melt bones. Plus, there was something about him, a deep graciousness, that went with beautifully manicured hands, the perfect haircut, the fresh-shaven face. Despite the khakis and sport shirt, this was not your ordinary *let's check out the hiking and fishing* type of man who spent a week with his guy friends in the mountainous Oregon village.

"Have a seat anywhere," Sophie invited them. "We don't offer dinner—we're just a day café. We close at three o'clock. But we have a great breakfast. I'll bring menus. Unless you want to look at the display case?"

"Menus, thank you." Again, it was the younger one who spoke.

Sophie nearly tripped over herself in her eagerness to get the men menus as they took a table by the window. Maddie ordered herself to get busy. Still, even as she filled cream pitchers, she was aware of that man, reluctantly feeling as if she had been given an irresistible reprieve from the worries that crowded her waking moments.

"So, in what exciting part of the world is it dinnertime

right now?" Sophie was back. She hugged the menus to herself instead of giving them out.

The big man looked at her, irritated at Sophie's question. His look clearly said, *Mind your own business.*

"Scotland," the other said, flashing Sophie an easy smile.

Maddie felt her heart dip at, not just the perfect teeth, but the natural sexiness in that smile, a heat that continued to his eyes, making the sapphire in them more intense.

"I thought so," Sophie said sagely, as if she was a world expert on dialects. "I detected a certain *Braveheart* in the accent. Your car is dreamy. I'm Sophie. And you are?"

Maddie put down the cream. "Sophie, if I could see you?" Obviously, she was going to have to give a lecture on being a little more professional. Dreamy car and introductions, indeed.

"In a sec," Sophie called.

"I'm Ward," the younger man, the one with the amazing presence, said easily.

The other said nothing.

"Lancaster," Ward filled in for him, giving him a look that might have suggested he be friendlier.

"Lancaster, are you by chance a policeman?"

Both men's eyebrows shot up.

Really, Maddie needed to step in, to stop this inquisition of customers, to take this opportunity to brief Sophie on professionalism, yes, even here in Mountain Bend. But if Sophie found out what Lancaster did, wouldn't it follow that Ward might volunteer what he did, as well?

There was something about him that was so intriguing, some power and mystery in the way he carried and conducted himself, that he had made Maddie aware there was a whole world out there that did not involve baking scones, fretting about bills, or watching helplessly as your world fell apart and your hometown declined around you.

Ridiculous to feel as if hope shimmered in the air around a complete stranger.

Because wasn't hope, after all, the most dangerous thing of all?

That, Maddie told herself, was the only thing she needed to know about the man who had entered the little main street coffee shop.

Not that he was a reprieve from a life that had gone heavy with worries.

No, that he was the exact opposite. That all her worries would intensify if she followed this lilting melody humming to life in the base of her being—the one that coincided with his appearance—to where it wanted to go.

She touched the gold chain on her neck. It was a pendant made with a gold nugget that her father had found a long time ago and given to her mother. Touching the pendant usually had the effect of grounding her. Sometimes, Maddie even imagined her father's voice when she touched it.

What would he say, right now, if he were here and saw her in such a ridiculous state over a man she had only just laid eyes on, to whom she had not even spoken a single word?

Something, she was sure, practical and homespun. *Whoa, girl, go easy.*

But she did not hear her father's voice, not even in her imagination. Instead, the pendant seemed to glow warm under her fingertips.

CHAPTER TWO

"LANCASTER DOES HAVE a military background, to be sure. What would you recommend from the menu?" It was Ward who spoke, his tone easy, but for the first time it seemed he would like to close the conversation with the young waitress

"Does Scotland have an army?" Sophie asked, nonplussed. "I wouldn't have thought—"

"Sophie, would you please give those gentlemen their menus, and then I need to talk to you for a minute?"

Ward turned and smiled at her and his smile was charismatic and sympathetic, as if he entirely got that training young employees was a little like trying to train an overly enthusiastic puppy.

Sophie surrendered the menus in slow motion. "What brings you to Mountain Bend?"

"We've come from a few days' holiday in California," Ward answered. "We're finishing up our stay in America with the Ritz concert."

The Ritz were a world-renowned band. Kettle's nephew, Sophie's cousin, was the drummer. It had been Kettle's idea for the band to officially open the summer season with a huge outdoor concert tomorrow night.

The hope was, once they had sampled the pristine charms of Mountain Bend, the throngs of people who had purchased tickets for the concert would return. Plan vacations here. Buy some of the empty miner's houses for summer cottages. Spend money on coffee and groceries and gas. Save the town.

It was a long shot, at best, but Maddie baked a back supply of scones, and printed off dozens of business cards, just in case.

"Well, the locals know the best sights," Sophie declared. "I'd be happy to show you around."

"Sophie!"

"After work," Sophie amended reluctantly.

Lancaster handed her his menu and folded his massive arms over his chest. "I'll have the Bend-in-the-Road."

"I think you'd prefer the Mountain Man," Sophie said sweetly.

"Could I see you for a moment?" Maddie called sternly and urgently.

Sophie ignored her. "Or maybe a few scones? That would make you feel right at home, wouldn't it?"

"If I wanted to feel at home," Lancaster said coolly, "I would have stayed there. And it's pronounced scone, as in gone, not scone, as in cone."

"I love a man who knows his scones," Sophie said, not insulted.

"I want the Bend-in-the-Road. I'm pretty sure I cannot get an edible scone in Mountain Bend, Oregon."

Maddie was pretty sure he was given a little nudge under the table with the other's foot.

"They happen to be the most delicious scones in the world," Sophie said loyally. "Maddie could have had a shop in New York someday, but—"

This was going seriously off the rails!

"Sophie!" Maddie called again, before it developed into an argument or a tell-all about Maddie's broken dreams and bad boyfriend.

Still, she could not help but be annoyed. You couldn't

get a good scone in Mountain Bend? That was a challenge if she had ever heard one!

Sophie gave her a disgruntled look, and the customers a reluctant one. "Sorry," she said. "Duty calls."

But then, before duty asked too much of Sophie, she leaned both elbows on the table, put her chin on her hands and blinked at Lancaster.

"So, do you ever wear a kilt?" she purred.

The big man looked stunned. After an initial moment of shocked silence, Ward threw back his head and laughed. If he'd been gorgeous before, it was now evident that had just been the warm-up. His laughter was pure, exquisitely masculine, entirely sexy.

Danger, Maddie reminded herself firmly.

Before Lancaster could answer, Sophie giggled, straightened up from the table and headed over to Maddie.

"What do you think?" she asked in a happy undertone. "Match, game and set to me?"

What she thought was that she envied Sophie's relative innocence. The younger woman thought you could play at this game with no one getting hurt. Both those men had a masculine potency about them that spoke of experience.

No doubt both of them had a string of broken hearts in their pasts. She didn't care if the assessment was completely unfair. It was better safe than sorry, and Sophie was a naive small-town girl.

Just as she herself had been when she met Derek. Maddie felt, again, protective of the younger woman.

"This is not how you interact with customers," she said, firmly. "You do not flirt with them. These shenanigans will end now."

"Shenanigans?" Sophie asked.

"A kilt?" Maddie demanded in an undertone.

"Don't say you don't want to know the answer," Sophie

said, grinning impishly, unintimidated by the neighbor she had known her whole life.

Maddie made to deny it. Her mouth opened. But her gaze, of its own accord, slid back to Ward. His strong, tanned legs were tucked under the table. A kilt? Good grief! She could feel herself beginning to blush!

Sophie laughed knowingly.

"Look," Maddie said, pulling herself together, "you're being way too inquisitive. They're customers. They're here for breakfast, not to exchange life stories. And they're not Americans. They won't appreciate your friendliness."

Sophie pursed her lips together, miffed at the reprimand, as Maddie had known she would be.

"Or apparently your scones," she said, pronouncing it as *gone* rather than *cone* as Maddie always had. Then she flounced through the swinging doors into the kitchen and gave Kettle the order.

"We ain't open yet." This declaration was followed by a string of cusswords used creatively and representing a long military history. "I don't make exceptions. And that includes the apron. And tie your hair back. We have standards." He put enough curse words between *have* and *standards* to impress a sailor.

Sure enough, Kettle himself stomped through the kitchen door. Despite the scowl on his grizzled face, Maddie felt a rush of affection.

Kettle had been her father's best friend, there for her and her mother when her father had been killed in a logging accident. He'd been there for her again as her mother, heartbroken, had followed on her father's heels way too quickly, leaving Maddie an orphan at eighteen.

Maddie's fiancé, Derek, had not gotten it when she had felt compelled to return to Mountain Bend after Kettle's accident, to manage the café. This was the code she had been raised with: you did right by the people who had done right by you.

So Kettle's stomp was a good thing. He was nearly back to his normal self after he had fallen off the restaurant roof while shoveling snow in the winter and had a complicated break to his hip that had required several surgeries.

Kettle had spent a military career he would not talk about with Delta Force before returning to Mountain Bend. Now he skidded to a halt, surveyed the two men with a certain bemused expression, and then turned back to the kitchen in time to intercept Sophie, who was coming out behind him.

"Maddie," he said gruffly, "you handle them customers. Sophie, you can help me in the kitchen for now."

Sophie looked as if she planned to protest, but she knew better than to argue with her uncle, especially her first day of working for him. She cast one last longing look at the table before reluctantly obeying and going back into the kitchen.

"I trust you to be sensible," Kettle told Maddie in an undertone. In other words, he trusted she'd outgrown the kind of shenanigans that got small-town girls, like her and Sophie, in all kinds of trouble.

Yes, she thought with a sigh, she was the sensible one *now*.

"I'm sure you won't be imagining anyone in kilts, or any other romantic nonsense, either."

So, he had heard something of that. She hoped she wasn't blushing, again, but Kettle wasn't looking at her, but watching their first guests of the day with narrowed eyes.

"What did they say they're doing here?" he asked quietly.

"The Ritz concert."

"The big one's security. Written all over him. Maybe doing an assessment before the band arrives."

"What about the other one?" Maddie asked, keeping her tone casual.

"Well, that's the odd part."

"In what way?"

"He looks like the principal, to me."

"The what?"

"Never mind. My old life creeps up on me, sometimes. I'm sure they are exactly what they say they are."

But he didn't sound sure at all.

"Like a school principal?" Maddie asked, unwilling, for some reason, to let it go.

Kettle snorted. "Does he look like a school principal to you?"

Maddie looked at him one more time, that subtle aura of power and confidence. "No," she admitted.

"Exactly. Someone who travels with a close protection specialist. Interesting."

Interesting enough to make Kettle stop from tossing them out before regular opening hours. He had definitely recognized something that had automatically given them his respect—generally hard earned—but that had also made him cautious about exposing his man-crazy niece to them.

"A close protection specialist?"

"A bodyguard in civilian terms. Never mind. I'm being silly." Kettle shook his head and went back to the kitchen muttering, "Ah, once a warrior."

The ancient coffeemaker let out a loud hiss, announcing the coffee was ready, and Maddie went and grabbed the pot.

She popped her head in the kitchen door. "Sophie, can you hand me some mugs from the dishwasher?"

Sophie brought over the mugs. "I know what their car looks like," she said in a hushed tone as she handed Maddie two thick crockery-style coffee mugs. "I'll bet they're staying at the Cottages. I'm going to go look as soon as I'm done with work."

She already was planning to thwart Kettle's plan to protect her!

"You will not," Maddie said.

Feeling uncomfortably in the middle of something, Maddie started to take the mugs and the pot over to the window table. Then she paused and picked up two scones from the display and set them on a plate.

"Coffee?" she asked. She set down the scones. "Complimentary. The grill isn't quite heated yet. Breakfast will be a few minutes."

While Lancaster eyed the scones with deep suspicion, and even prodded one with his finger, it was Ward who answered, and again she had a sense of him being in a leadership position.

Did he do something that warranted a bodyguard? It seemed a little far-fetched for Mountain Bend. Poor Kettle just hadn't been himself since he fell off that roof.

"Thank you. I'm Ward and this is Lancaster. And you are?"

She actually blushed, but kept her tone deliberately cool. "It's Sophie's first day. I hope she didn't give you the impression it's some kind of American tradition for staff at restaurants to introduce themselves to customers."

"It isn't? Lancaster, didn't we have that happen before? In Los Angeles? That fellow. Franklin! He definitely introduced himself. *Hi, I'm Franklin, and I'll be your server tonight.*"

"You're right," she conceded. "It is protocol at some of the big chains. But here in Mountain Bend, not so much."

"Thank you for clarifying that," Ward said. "I find learning another country's customs a bit like learning a new language. There's lots of room for innocent error. But now you have us at a disadvantage. You know our names, but we are none the wiser."

She frowned. She was aware of *needing* to keep distance between her and this powerfully attractive sample of manliness. Still, she could not see a way out of it. Asking him to call her Miss Nelson would be way too stilted.

"Madeline," she said, and it sounded stilted anyway and somehow unfriendly. "Maddie," she amended in an attempt to soften it a bit.

"Maddie."

Just as she had feared, her name coming off his lips in that sensual accent was as if he had touched the nape of her neck with his fingertips.

"I can't help but notice your pendant. It's extraordinary." He reached up, and for a moment they both froze, anticipation in the air between them.

Then he touched it, ever so lightly. The pendant suddenly felt hot, almost as though there would be a scorch mark on her neck where it rested.

Maddie shivered, from the bottom of her toes to the top of her head.

CHAPTER THREE

"BEAUTIFUL," WARD SAID SOFTLY. He withdrew his hand, his amazing sapphire eyes intent on her face.

The pronouncement could mean the pendant. But it could also mean—

"A gold nugget?" he asked her.

Obviously, he meant the pendant! Maddie had to pull herself together! Good grief. She felt as though she was trembling.

"Y-y-yes, my father found it and had it made into this piece."

"Lovely," he said, and again, it felt as if he might be commenting on more than the pendant. "My name's a diminutive, too. Short for Edward."

Did Lancaster shake his head, ever so slightly?

Ward changed tack so effortlessly that Maddie wondered if she had imagined that slight shake of head.

"Do you live up to it?" Ward asked in that sexy brogue. He took a sip of the freshly poured coffee and his laughing eyes met hers over the rim of the cup.

"Excuse me?"

"Your name? Are you mad?"

She wondered if, in her attempts to remain professional, she had ended up looking cranky! That was the thing to remember about men like this. Even simple things were complicated around them. She tried to relax her features as she realized he was deliberately trying to tease some of the stiffness from her.

She remembered Kettle's confidence that she would be sensible. But not stiff and uninviting, even if it was self-protective. And suddenly she didn't feel like living up to Kettle's stodgy expectation of her.

"Mad, angry or mad, crazy?" Maddie asked him, returning his smile tentatively. It was an indicator of how serious everything in her life had become that she considered engaging in this banter and returning his smile living dangerously.

"Obviously, neither," he said, saluting her with his coffee cup.

Was he flirting? With her? That certainly upped the chances of the mad, crazy. Especially if she engaged with him. Of course, she wouldn't engage!

Or any other romantic nonsense. Though she suddenly felt a need not just to defy Kettle's impressions of her, but to have a moment of lightness.

"And do you live up to your name?" she asked him.

He raised an eyebrow at her.

"Do you ward?"

"Ward, protect?" he asked her. "Or ward, admit to the hospital?"

They shared a small ripple of laughter, that appreciation that comes when you come across someone who thinks somewhat the same way you do. Their eyes met, and a spark, like an ember escaped from a bonfire, leaped between them.

Maddie reminded herself that one spark, even that small, could burn down a whole forest. She'd had her moment, Maddie told herself, clinging to the sensibility Kettle was relying on her for.

"Ward off pesky waitresses, I hope," Lancaster said darkly, and then before she could take it personally, "Where's your friend?"

"Her uncle needed her in the kitchen."

"Locked her up," Lancaster muttered with approval. He took a scone off the plate and scowled at it. "Is this a flavor?"

"Yes, it has a hint of orange in it."

"There's no flavors in scones," Lancaster said firmly. "Do you have cream?"

"Cream? For the coffee? Of course. I'll go get it."

"No, for the scones. Cornish cream?"

"Sorry, I—"

"Too much to hope for." He took a gigantic bite. And then, to Maddie's satisfaction, he sighed and closed his eyes. "That's good. Even without cream. Try it," he insisted to Ward.

Ward picked up the other scone and took a bite. Even that small gesture spoke of refinement. There was that ultrasexy smile again. "You owe somebody an apology," he told Lancaster. "Not only edible, but possibly the best scone this side of the Atlantic."

"Any side of the Atlantic." Lancaster finished the scone in two bites and eyed Ward's hungrily.

"Who made these?" Ward asked, polishing it off.

"I did."

"You did not. You've got to have a Celt hiding in that kitchen." Again, Ward was teasing her, as if he sensed she took life altogether too seriously.

Maybe it was weakness to engage, and to want to engage, but what the heck? The men would eat their breakfast and be gone. They might come back, or she might see them in the street and wave, but it was hardly posting banns at the local church. After the concert tomorrow night, they would disappear, never to be seen again.

Unless they bought one of the old miner's cottages. Unless they fell in love with Mountain Bend.

She did not want to be thinking of falling in love, in any of its many guises, anywhere in the vicinity of the very appealing Ward!

"It's an old family recipe," Maddie supplied. "My grandmother was English. And she pronounced it scone, as in cone."

"Two strikes," Lancaster muttered.

"Both entirely forgivable," Ward said. "Do you think I could bother you for another for my hungry friend?"

Maddie brought back a plate of scones and Ward asked, "So it was you who was going to have a shop in New York City?"

"If I was, it was a long way in the future. Anyway, New York City is in my past now." She needed to move on. She had just lectured Sophie about professionalism. There was no fraternizing with the customers!

She stood there, paralyzed.

"We visited briefly, before we went to California," Ward volunteered. "This seems preferable to me, the little piece of America everyone knows exists, but that is hard to find. I work in community-based economies. I'd be interested to learn more about your town."

She cocked her head at him. His intelligence and genuine interest was pulling at her. He was definitely a man she would love to sit down and have a conversation with.

And of course she was not going to give in to that temptation!

"I'd love to talk to you," she said, and unfortunately, she meant it. "Maybe we'll get together sometime."

That part she did not mean at all!

"Can I get you something else?" she said quickly, a reminder to all involved what kind of relationship this was.

"Tea would be wonderful."

She brought tea and more scones to their table, but thankfully it was opening time, so she could not linger. There was a surprising number of people coming into the café. The town appeared to be benefiting already from people arriving for tomorrow's concert.

Was it possible this was going to work?

She didn't have time to contemplate it for long. Her life became a whirlwind as Sophie remained in the kitchen. Kettle delivered the two men breakfast, but Maddie did not interact with them again until it was time to take their money at the till.

"You know how to make tea, too," Ward said. "That's a rare gift in this country!"

A small thing, not worthy of a blush, and yet there she was, blushing over tea! Or maybe it was the fact that his hand had brushed hers, and she had felt the jolt of his pure presence, the same way she had when his finger had rested, ever so briefly, on the pendant at her neck.

"That English granny again," she said.

"Somehow the last thing I think of when I look at you is an English granny," he said, his voice a sexy rasp. Then he looked faintly taken aback, as if he had said something wildly inappropriate. He recovered quickly, though.

"I hope we do have a chance to talk about your town's transition," Ward said. He said it as if he was talking to someone whose opinion he would respect. She glanced at him. Small talk.

"Me, too," she said with bright insincerity. "Enjoy your stay here."

Then she snapped the cash register shut and whirled away from them, feeling somehow as if she had escaped some unknowable danger.

Why would such a feeling, the feeling of a near miss on a road named Catastrophe, be tinged with regret?

* * *

"That was a good breakfast," Lancaster said, as they exited the coffee shop. "You've got to give it to Yanks. They know how to eat. The scones were a surprise of the best possible sort."

"Are you saying barracks food doesn't appeal?"

"No, Your Highness."

Both men looked around, but no one was within hearing.

"Sorry, sir, lifetime habits are hard to break."

They came to the car and Ward regarded it appreciatively. "Do you want to drive, Major Lancaster?" He glanced around. "You're right about lifetime habits."

"I was hoping for an opportunity. Where to?"

"I feel, after California and New York, I just need to stretch my legs and have some space. What about those hot pools we heard about?"

"The hotel clerk told us they were in the middle of the wilderness," Lancaster said, appalled.

"That part of America interests me."

"I think this is bear country," Lancaster said doubtfully, the quandary written on his face. How to keep the Prince safest?

"I'm prepared to live dangerously."

"I was afraid of that." Lancaster looked less than pleased, for he was a man born into the station of guarding the royal family of the Isle of Havenhurst, and he sniffed out—and avoided—situations that might place the Prince in danger, but he also knew an order when he heard it.

"The cover story went well," Ward said as they left Mountain Bend and took a rough road that began to twist up the mountain through thick forest.

Lancaster was silent.

"Didn't you think so?"

"The old guy didn't buy it."

"What old guy?"

"He came out of the kitchen for a minute and gave us a good look over. Limping. Ex-military."

"How can you tell that?"

Lancaster shrugged. "There are ways to tell. But it works both ways. I think he could tell a bit about us, too."

Ward contemplated the fact he had not registered the man coming out of the kitchen. Of course, it was Lancaster's job to notice who was around them, and Ward was confident Lancaster was probably better at his job than just about anybody in the world. But still, Ward suspected the woman, Maddie, had something to do with the fact he had not noticed the man come out of the kitchen.

There was something about her that engaged him, especially after coming from California, where the women he met all seemed very outgoing, very tall, very tanned, wrinkle-free and white-blond.

In contrast he had found Maddie's beauty was understated and natural, as refreshing as a cool breeze on a warm day. She was lovely, with those kissed-by-the-sun curls springing around her head, her delicate features, the perfect bow of puffy lips, hazel eyes that looked green one moment and doe brown the next. Despite the faintest hint of freckles, unlike her California counterparts, her skin had been porcelain pale, as if, despite being surrounded by the outdoors, she did not get outside much. And there had been faint shadows of what—weariness? worry?—under those remarkable eyes.

In their short encounter Ward had found her both delightfully interesting and intriguingly attractive, and at the same time a painful reminder of the kind of woman and kind of life he would never have.

"I'm not concerned. Yet," Lancaster said. "But I wouldn't be telling anyone else your name is Edward."

"Havenhurst is probably the least known kingdom in the entire North Atlantic, a little speck in the ocean, two hundred kilometers from the North Channel. Even the Scots, who are the most culturally linked to us, barely know who we are. So, few people know who I am."

Ward's publicity-averse family employed a small army to fend off the pursuit of royalty-crazed tabloids, and though the odd picture or story about him emerged, he was mostly an unknown.

Lancaster looked unconvinced.

"I'm off the radar," Ward assured him.

"Best to keep it that way. I think your California friend, Miss O'Brian, would have loved to have milked your status for a bit of publicity."

Ward gave Lancaster a look. "Did you give her a talking-to?"

Lancaster lifted a huge shoulder. "Laid out a few ground rules, aye."

The road had ended. Lancaster turned off the car, and they got out. They removed day packs from the trunk and hoisted them onto shoulders.

Hours later, they returned to the car. They had hiked all day, but they had not succeeded in finding the hot pool.

"The more we didn't find them, the more I was homesick for a dip," Ward said. "Maybe we should take that young waitress up on her offer to show us the sights, after all."

"Huh. With a chaperone, maybe."

"Perhaps Maddie could join us, too."

"I don't think that's a good idea," Lancaster offered.

Ward shot Lancaster a look. Had he guessed there

was something about the gamine scone enchantress that had piqued his interest? But no, the scowl said something else entirely.

"Because the young Sophie may have been a bit smitten with you?"

Lancaster scowled. "Emphasis on *young*. There's bound to be a slipup. Questions asked that can't be answered. The cover story won't stand up to close scrutiny."

Ward reminded himself it was Lancaster's job to think like this, to be on the alert for potential threats and possible dangers, real and imagined.

But he realized wanting Maddie and Sophie to join them wasn't just about finding the hot pools. Maddie, with her curls and her tentative smile, had made him long for something he knew he could not have. Or maybe he could, not forever, but for a few moments in time. Maybe these last few final days of anonymity could give him one chance to see what it was like to have fun with an ordinary girl in an ordinary world. He felt a need to articulate it.

"Please don't deprive me of this opportunity to do a few normal things, Lancaster. Yes, I want to drive a car like this one. But I want to laugh with a pretty lass. Dance at a concert. This may be the only opportunity I ever get to experience a normal life."

A normal life. They got back in the car and Ward took the driver's seat this time. Their small island home did not lend itself to a vehicle like this. In truth, he rarely drove himself anywhere. He put the car in gear and enjoyed the surge of power as he pressed down the gas. Lancaster made an unflattering grab for a bar above his door, but Edward soon found his groove and drove the car as quickly as the poor road would allow.

"I understand, Your Highness," Lancaster said. "This

is really your only taste of freedom. In a few weeks you'll be a married man."

"I've never had freedom," Ward said quietly, "married or not. Just the same, I've reached a decision. I've decided not to marry Princess Aida."

CHAPTER FOUR

"But…but your marriage is expected," Lancaster stammered, after a long silence.

"I've always understood that service comes before self, and that certain sacrifices would be expected of me."

"Princess Aida is a beautiful woman, sir, hardly a sacrifice."

"She doesn't love me."

"Love?" Lancaster shot him a distressed look. "What does that have to do with it?"

Love. Ward had never had an expectation of it in his life. His father, the King, had not loved his mother, nor she him. Their public lives had been orchestrated to be civil; privately they had been cold and distant to one another.

Ward himself had been sent away to a private school when he was six. So *love* was a nebulous thing to him. He had not experienced it, nor had any expectation of it.

Edward thought of Aida with affection, like one would think of a little sister. When she had come to him and told him she *loved* someone else, he had felt a shocking sense of envy for what was shining in her eyes.

And he'd felt the difficulty of what he needed to do. His nation wanted one thing. His family demanded one thing. His conscience commanded another. He could not be the one to kill the light that had shone from Aida when she talked about Drew Mooretown, the man on her personal guard that she now loved.

"The sacrifice would have been hers, if we married,"

Edward said slowly. "I've no notions of love. We've both known, since we were children, what was expected of us and what the benefit to both of our nations is. Like me, she'll do what's required of her, but, Lancaster, she loves another. I cannot do this to her."

"You're a good man," Lancaster said with a sigh, and Prince Edward Alexander the Fourth knew he had been paid the highest of compliments from one who rarely gave them. He could only hope it was true. "But it's not going to be as easy to get out of it as you think. Your father—"

"Would force it, I know."

"I don't relish the thought of marching you down the aisle with a sword at your back." Lancaster was only partly kidding. "What are you going to do? I've known this whole trip something was deeply troubling you. It seems impossible to get out of it. Unless you're thinking of not going back?"

"Rest easy, Lancaster. You don't have to feel a divided loyalty between your duty to your King and your duty to me. There will be no having to think of a way to wrestle me back to my kingdom. I have always known my destiny is there, and I embrace that. I love my work on economic development, bringing the island new ideas and prosperity, acting as a liaison with the people. I love listening to their ideas and concerns, involving them in the future of our island. I love Havenhurst."

"Then what?"

"I have to set Aida free. And I think there's only one way to do that where unbearable pressure wouldn't be brought on her."

"Which is?"

"I have to marry someone else. Before we return."

"Within days, in other words?"

"Yes."

"A kind of pretend marriage?"

"Yes, just long enough to enable Aida to go off and marry her chap without the indignation of two kingdoms being heaped on her."

"Being heaped on you, instead."

"I have broad shoulders. After it has all died down, a quiet annulment could be arranged."

Lancaster was silent but then spoke. "But you would have to marry genuinely, eventually. Marriage is expected."

Yes, it was expected that Edward would marry, and that out of that marriage would come that all-important heir to the royal legacy.

Not expected: that he would ever know the kind of love he had seen shining in Aida's face when she had confessed to him that she had met another.

Not expected: a longing for this thing his position would probably keep him from ever knowing.

Not expected: that a man the world would see as having absolutely everything—wealth and power beyond the dreams of most mortals—would feel this odd emptiness. A sense of missing something that had increased every day they had explored America, been normal, been free of Havenhurst.

"Perhaps I won't marry at all."

"That sounds a lonely life."

"Will you marry again, Lancaster?" Ward asked softly, remembering the man Lancaster used to be, a man who had radiated a kind of faith in the goodness of life.

"I don't think so," Lancaster said, looking off into the distance. "A man's heart can only take so much."

Lancaster's wife and young baby had been killed in a cottage fire. Lancaster had been away at a training program off-island when it had happened. The whole island had mourned the loss of his family, and five years later, Lancaster still carried an aura of deep mourning about him.

Mourning, mingled with a kind of steadfast, put-one-foot-in-front-of-the-other strength.

"No, I won't marry again," he said. "Not while there are streams that need fishing. But you...you'll be expected to find a wife."

There was the weight of all those expectations again.

"My position makes it more difficult to find a partner, not less."

Lancaster snorted. "Once you are seen as available, women will be throwing themselves at you, Your Highness."

"Not at me," Ward said, and could hear the weariness in his own voice. "At the fantasy of being a princess. At the role they think I play. At their impossible romantic ideas. The reality is so different. The obligations that go with the title would place an unfair burden on someone not brought up in it."

"There is the little issue of an heir," Lancaster reminded him. "You will be King."

"My sister is married, and they have dear, sweet Anne. Perhaps one day she will reign."

"She's a girl!"

"The times are changing, Lancaster."

Lancaster looked dubious about that, at least in the context of Havenhurst. "You've given this some thought."

"I have, indeed."

"How do you find someone to play the role of a pretend princess? It's not as if you can put an ad in the personal section of the newspaper. *Prince in search of bride.*"

"I've asked Sea O'Brian."

They had just spent several days with Sea at her villa in California. Ward had met the actress at a party, a long time ago, on a yacht in the Mediterranean. He had not developed a taste for such things, but he and the famous actress had kept in touch.

Lancaster was silent.

"You don't approve?"

"It's not my place to approve or disapprove of your choices, sir."

"My thought was that she was an actress already. She could play it like a role. And the publicity would certainly benefit her career. I'd like whoever takes this on to benefit in some way. I think the deception of a nation—not to mention my father and mother—is a great deal to ask of an individual."

Again, Lancaster was silent, but his brows had lowered and he was looking straight ahead with such fierce concentration that it could only mean disapproval. They had known each other so long and spent so much time together there was an unbreakable bond between them, almost as if they were brothers.

"I'm interested in your thoughts."

Lancaster took a deep breath. "As you say, sir, she's an actress. There always seems to be lots of drama unfolding around her. I overheard her talking to her press secretary about alerting a tabloid to your presence at her villa and had to head her off."

Ward had not been aware of any of this, an indication of how well Lancaster did his job, and how seriously he took it.

"I don't imagine Sea O'Brian is easy to *head off*," he said mildly.

"Correct," Lancaster said.

"How did you manage it?"

"I took her cell phone hostage," Lancaster admitted reluctantly. "Her *life*, as she told me. She'd been snapping pictures of you when you weren't aware. Anyway, all this leads me to believe that trying to extricate yourself from the situation could get very complicated."

"True," Ward conceded.

"The people won't like her," Lancaster said, his voice low. "They'll see her as glib and superficial. She's not of the earth."

This was a highest form of praise in Havenhurst: he or she is of the earth.

There was a grave silence between the two men, and when Lancaster spoke, his tone was faintly lighter.

"Perhaps you could consider that lass from the café this morning. Think of the scones!" Lancaster crowed. Now that they were alone, he pronounced it *skoons* in the language of their island kingdom.

Both men laughed.

"I think there is far less danger of damage hiring an actress to play the role of my wife than to involve an ordinary girl living her ordinary life," Ward said firmly.

He had found a way to save Aida, without hurting anyone else, or his island kingdom. He was satisfied with his choice. The truth was a woman like Maddie, from the little time he had spent with her, deserved things he could not give.

Love, for one.

That was a topic he knew nothing about. Nothing. Love would be for him, as it had been for his parents, the great unknown. His parents had done precisely what he would do—they had sacrificed any chance of personal happiness for what they saw as the good of Havenhurst.

And he would do the same. Love was not part of his duty, nor his destiny, and he had known those truths forever. He had made a decision to save Aida from this same lonely fate, and that was good enough.

Even though Ward had decided the scone enchantress

was not marriage material—she might already be married for all he knew—he had a feeling that if he wanted to glimpse normal, to feel it and be it for these few days of freedom remaining to him, she could show him that. It would be even better if she had a husband or a boyfriend. They could give him a glimpse of that tantalizing thing called *normal* together.

"Why don't we go see if Maddie and Sophie are willing to show us the pool?" Ward suggested after a moment.

"I still don't think it's a good idea."

"Maddie might even have—what do they call it here? A significant other! Who could come with us."

Lancaster cast him a long look and finally, reluctantly, nodded.

"We're just getting ready to close," Maddie said when the bell rang over the door. She was exhausted. The day had been frantically busy, visitors already thronging the town for tomorrow's concert. She would not be attending the concert. She preferred a warm bath and a good book.

She glanced up and froze.

It was the two men from this morning, Ward and Lancaster.

"Are there scones left?" Lancaster asked without preamble.

"Is that panic I hear in your voice?" Ward asked. He smiled at Maddie. "It takes a lot to panic him. Please tell him you have scones left. Hello, by the way. Nice to see you again."

He said it as if he really meant it.

"You, too," she said, and then wished she hadn't, because she really meant it, too, only she probably really meant it way more than he really meant it.

"If we've dispensed with the social niceties?" Lancaster prodded.

Exactly! Social niceties. Meaningless. Not that she wanted them to have meaning. She was done with that kind of thing. The thrill of a handsome man. The excitement of getting to know someone. The feeling of being close. The tingle of hands touching. That incredible sensation of being alive.

She was done with it—but she was aware she longed for it, too. She had told herself she remained in Mountain Bend, after Derek's betrayal, because she was needed here.

But couldn't that be a way of hiding?

And now, what she was hiding from appeared to have found her. It was like a chocolate addict giving up bonbons. It was all well and good until someone waved one under your nose.

"Do any scones remain?" Lancaster asked plaintively.

See? She was already drifting off, contemplating the many missed pleasures of bonbons. She drew herself up short.

"Unfortunately, no," she said. "We've had crowds. Once I added the Cornish cream, I couldn't keep up with the demand."

"You said you didn't have any!"

"You're making the poor man swoon," Ward pointed out good-naturedly.

She dared not look at him. If he was smiling, and she knew he was—she could tell by the added lilt in his voice—she might be the one swooning!

"I looked up some recipes. It's really just whipped cream, but done until it's very nearly butter, yes?"

"Will you marry me?" Lancaster asked. "And if not me, him?"

Despite her vow not to look, she cast a startled glance

at Ward, thinking he would be laughing uproariously. Why did Ward not seem to think that was funny?

"Anyway, we sold out, but I have some in the freezer I could get for you."

"Perhaps a dozen? And as much cream as you're willing to part with."

"You'll get fat," a voice behind him said. "They're made with pure butter. And then whipped cream, too? Your arteries won't thank you. It's a disgraceful way to treat a beautiful body."

Lancaster whirled and glared at Sophie. "I'll thank you not to comment on my arteries. My body is not your business, either."

"We could change that," Sophie purred.

"We couldn't," Lancaster snapped firmly, much to Maddie's relief. What was Sophie doing, talking to a virtual stranger like that?

"Mountain Bend is a beautiful place," Ward said conversationally to Maddie as she returned with frozen scones and packed them in a box. "Our part of the world has some beautiful places, to be sure, but nothing quite this untamed. Sophie mentioned the best sights were known by the locals. Would you say that's true?"

Maddie nodded, feeling oddly wary.

"Do you think maybe you could show us some? When you're all wrapped up here? You and the delightful Miss Sophie?"

Maddie felt herself freeze. Did Ward like Sophie? Well, who could blame him? And why did she care? It felt like this treacherous attraction she felt for him had to be quelled immediately. But still, Maddie looked over her shoulder at him, and he was smirking at Lancaster with a certain devilment in his smile. He turned back to her and winked.

Winked!

Immediately, she ordered herself to say no to this. She was not up to a man who could make such a simple thing as a playful wink seem sexy. But somehow that simple word stuck in her throat and would not come out.

"Lancaster and I spent the day trying to find a hot pool," Ward said, "and despite having a map we did not turn it up."

"Honeymoon Hot Springs," Sophie said, excited as a puppy who had been shown a toy. "How did you hear about those? It's Mountain Bend's best-kept secret."

"Someone at our hotel told us."

That was unusual, but he *was* charming. He probably just had to smile to get poor old Adele, who worked the front desk at the Cottages, to want immediately to impress him with all the secrets the locals guarded from outsiders. Even now, when they were desperately trying to attract tourists, Honeymoon Hot Springs was rarely mentioned. The name said it all—it was so special to people here. A favorite place for wedding proposals, romantic interludes, honeymoon nights. It was a place couples went for privacy. It was absolutely the wrong place to go with a man you felt the slightest attraction to!

"Naturally, we'd want your, uh, significant other, to come, as well," Ward said.

"She doesn't have one!" Sophie said, like someone in possession of a piece of juicy gossip they couldn't wait to share. "Her fiancé was the world's biggest jerk."

Maddie gave Sophie a look that could kill.

"Well, he was," Sophie said, somehow missing the look entirely. "She came home to look after Kettle, and guess what he did? With her best friend?"

Maddie was mortified. She stared at Sophie in shocked horror. They all stood there in embarrassed distress.

Too late, Sophie became aware of her gaffe. She turned stricken eyes to Maddie. "I didn't mean to—"

"Not to worry," Maddie said brightly. "I'm sorry, no. Local people don't like outsiders going there. I have things to do. Thank you for your interest, but I can't. I—"

"Of course, we'll show you," Sophie said, stubbornly, recovering way too quickly from divulging other people's private lives. She was obviously as thrilled by the men's interest in that secret place with its reputation for romantic enchantment, as Maddie was not.

"Sophie," she said. "It's—"

But Sophie cut her off with a toss of her thick black hair. "I will, if she won't."

There! Sophie had managed to make her sound like a terrible stick-in-the-mud. Had she become a terrible stick-in-the-mud? A person thrown over for another who could not get over it? She thought of her life since she'd returned to Mountain Bend. Work and worry.

She turned stiffly and handed the box of scones to Lancaster. "If there's anything else?" Yes, she recognized it. The voice of a stick-in-the-mud, a woman whose broken heart would no doubt lead her to spinsterhood.

It was what Kettle loved about her, she reminded herself!

But then, ever so naturally, Ward laid his hand across Maddie's wrist. His hand was warm and dry and his touch was firm. But more, his touch transmitted something of his power. She could feel the jolt of his substantial and seductive energy surge up the whole length of her arm.

It occurred to Maddie he was not a man accustomed to people saying no to him, which made it all the more imperative that she do exactly that!

"Please say yes," Ward said softly.

CHAPTER FIVE

MADDIE YANKED HER wrist out from under Ward's hand and resisted an impulse to rub it where it tingled.

Say no, she ordered herself.

Now she was pretty sure he was insisting out of pity. On the other hand, Sophie was going to do whatever she pleased, no matter how ill-advised it was. And playing with fire was ill-advised. Taking a man you barely knew to a place with a name like Honeymoon Hot Springs was playing with fire! Joining the excursion would not be the least bit sensible, which was Kettle's expectation of Maddie.

Really? Maddie thought this was a very bad idea. They did not know these two men. Of course they seemed charming, but you couldn't know these things from a short conversation. She watched true crime shows! And Honeymoon Hot Springs was a long way off the beaten track.

She cast a glance at the two men. It was a poor argument. Ward has asked if her *significant other* would like to join them. Besides, both men radiated decency, a kind of bone-deep honor.

The real reason she was reluctant was because she did not see the point of encouraging Sophie to get in any deeper with Lancaster. He was leaving; she was staying. And the same went for getting to know Ward any better. The hot springs, themselves, invited a kind of instant intimacy. Bathing suits! The romantic setting.

The whole idea had emotional catastrophe written all

over it. But she could tell Sophie was set on going, and she was not about to let her go alone, particularly since there would be bathing suits involved! Chaperoning Sophie might be the more *sensible* way of looking at it!

Besides, hadn't Maddie played it safe her whole life? Said no to every adventure? Scuttled away from every perceived danger? Had it, in any way, protected her from what life had planned?

It had not.

Besides, now, thanks to Sophie, she had to correct the impression that she was hiding away in Mountain Bend nursing a broken heart.

Which had enough elements of truth to it, that it suddenly felt imperative to make that correction.

Feeling as if she was standing on the rock ledge that jutted out way, way above Honeymoon Hot Springs, with that pool of deep turquoise steaming water far, far below, Maddie closed her eyes. *Jump?* Or walk away without ever knowing what adventure might have unfolded?

Maybe it wouldn't even be an adventure, just an ordinary excursion, getting to know someone a little better, saying, *See? I'm not broken.* Couldn't she just have fun? Wasn't it her who was attaching seriousness to the whole encounter that it did not need to have?

She had never jumped off that rock ledge, as some of the bolder people had done. It was time to take a chance, wasn't it?

"Okay," she said. "Yes."

Sophie whooped with surprised delight.

And Maddie noticed the exhaustion she had been feeling, just minutes ago, seemed to have evaporated.

"I'll have to go home and put on a bathing suit," Maddie said.

"A bathing suit?" Sophie said. "Usually we—"

Maddie gave her a look that could have stripped paint. "I don't know what you usually do, Sophie, but you won't be doing it today."

She sounded like a miffed schoolteacher. She turned back to the men. "Can we meet back here in an hour?"

Somehow, now that she had acted like a miffed schoolteacher, if felt imperative that she not *look* like one, like a stodgy chaperone, old and humorless before her time, there to spoil everyone's fun.

"Perfect."

As he was going out the door, Lancaster turned back to her. *Thank you*, he mouthed. Maddie was not sure if he meant for the scones, for her agreement to accompany them to the falls, or for her setting out dress restrictions.

Picking an outfit proved more difficult than she had imagined. The bathing suit was not a problem—she had only two, both black, one-piece and equally matronly.

But what to wear over top? Honeymoon Hot Springs was not exactly a walk in the park, but a hike with some steep and rocky terrain to traverse.

Aware of the ticking of the clock—what had made her say they would meet in an hour—Maddie showered and dressed. Several times. She finally settled on a pair of shorts, longer than the ones that Sophie was wearing today, but that still showed off the length of her legs. She put a blue plaid shirt over her bathing suit and knotted it at the waist. The outfit was completed with sturdy hiking shoes.

She put some product in her hair and scrunched up her curls, and then she added large hoop earrings that made her short hair look like she had actually planned the cut as an act of supreme self-confidence, not sheared it off because it was convenient and because she no longer cared to be attractive!

After debating a moment—the hot springs did not really lend themselves to makeup—Maddie dusted her nose with a bit of makeup to hide her freckles and then added some waterproof mascara and just a touch of shadow. She used a color that made her eyes appear more green than brown. One thing about the hair, she decided, giving herself one more quick once-over in the mirror before she headed out the door, was it made her eyes look huge. In fact, she was pleased to see she looked quite pretty. She realized, surprised, she had just enjoyed the rituals of being feminine again. She felt as if she was going on a date. Was she going on a date?

Her hand went to the pendant on her neck, as it so often did when she was uncertain. What would her father think of her going to the hot springs with a stranger? Surely, he wouldn't approve?

But when she closed her eyes and pictured him, he was smiling. *Life is so short*, he said. *Don't be afraid to be bold.*

Maddie opened her eyes, and looked at herself one more time. Maybe there was just a hint of her father's boldness in her.

Every bit of the extra time she had taken felt worth it when she saw Ward's eyes light up with appreciation when they met again in front of the café.

Seeing Sophie's outfit—even shorter shorts than earlier in the day and a crocheted cover-up over a very colorful but skimpy bikini top—Maddie thought she and Sophie should ride in the back of the car together.

But Ward opened the front door of the vehicle for her and nodded at the scowling Lancaster to get in the back with Sophie. Lancaster looked less than pleased about the arrangement and turned so he faced out the window.

As they roared up the mountain road, Maddie relaxed

her need to be in control. In fact, it reminded Maddie of those carefree days of being a teenager. Not the car, of course, but the *feeling*. Bold. Embracing the everyday adventures that were offered.

The trailhead was not visible from the road, especially at this time of year, with the shrubs leafed in. Behind the leafy shrubs, the beginning of the trails was marked with a single wooden post with no markings on it. There were colorful rings around the bottom of it, and Maddie slid a blue one up to the top and hung it on a nail there.

"What does that mean?" Ward asked, curious.

"It will alert others to the fact there are people in the pools, but it's blue, so it means anyone is welcome, and that certain—"

She cast Sophie a meaningful look, which Sophie ignored.

"Certain conventions will be respected. The pink ring would mean someone is in there who wants privacy, and the yellow would mean others are welcome but whoever is in there is without a bathing suit."

She blushed when she said it.

"I think it may be fortuitous that Lancaster and I didn't find our way earlier," Ward said with a smile.

"You may be right," Maddie agreed, returning his smile.

Within a few minutes of being on the trail to the hot pools, Maddie wondered how she could have possibly envisioned catastrophe of any kind. A well-beaten dirt trail, wide enough for two people to walk abreast, wound its way through the shady groves of old-growth forest. The light filtered, green and gold, through the thick canopy, and she could smell the heady perfume of pine and cedar needles being crushed underfoot, and the headier perfume of Ward: clean, male, earthy.

"I'm not sure how we missed this when we looked earlier," Ward said. "I may have to surrender my Boy Scout badge in woodsmanship."

"They have Boy Scouts in Scotland?" Maddie asked. Did he hesitate ever so slightly before he answered? No, she must have imagined it.

"Aye," he said, "and they wear kilts."

"They don't!"

"Scout's honor," he said, and they laughed easily together. Given her resistance to coming in the first place, it was terrible to be so glad that she had!

It had been a long time—way too long—since she had done anything just for fun. The walk to the pools, like the drive, reminded her of more-carefree days. The forest was a soothing, serene place.

Lancaster, carrying the huge picnic basket as effortlessly as if it was a doll's purse, strode up ahead, with Sophie having to skip along to keep up with him. This did not stop her breathless chatter from drifting back to them.

"I'm worried she's giving him entirely the wrong impression," Maddie confided in Ward. "She's acting as if she's far more worldly than she is."

"Don't worry," Ward said easily. "You will never meet a man with more honor than Lancaster. He sees her as a foolish young girl with a crush. He would never take advantage."

"Oh? Also Scout's honor?" Maddie asked.

"Something like that."

Again, she felt he was ever so deftly sidestepping something. But what? She chided herself for being way too serious, as always.

She was going to ask him a bit about where he came from and what he did for a living, but he beat her to it.

"Tell me a little about your town," he said.

This seemed like safe ground, conversationally.

"You said you know a little bit already."

"A little," he agreed.

"That transition you mentioned this morning? From resource based to tourist and ecology is not much more than a pipe dream at the moment. Many of the old-timers here resist the idea of tourists, even if it could save the town, and that's a big if. They see it as unspoiled around here. And they're protective of that. I think they'd rather let the town die a natural death than see a paved path into these springs, or a hotel sitting at the trailhead."

"That's understandable. What happened to the economy?"

"By the time I was born, the mine, the town's biggest employer had already shut down. There was still logging and a bit of trapping. They were dangerous, dirty professions—my dad was killed in a logging accident."

"I'm sorry," he said, with such genuine sympathy she felt an unexpected prick behind her eyelids. "I can see the pendant must have extra meaning for you. How old were you?"

"Sixteen."

He made a sound at the back of his throat, sympathetic and distressed, a man who wanted to protect others from the tragedies of life.

"The work in Mountain Bend attracted hardworking honest people who invested in the town. But now everyone's kind of watching helplessly as the town disintegrates a little more every year, and the only things they own, their houses and businesses, are becoming a little more worthless.

"There is a big hope that the Ritz concert will bring people here who wouldn't normally come. That they'll see what a special place it is and snap up some of the empty houses. If they did, businesses like the Black Kettle would be more viable, even if we could just have a summer season.

"I'm hoping the scones will take off. If people liked them enough, they might be willing to place online orders, though the logistics of shipping from here I haven't quite worked out. If we could attract a few people here who could work online..."

Her voice drifted away. She suddenly felt as if she was talking too much, almost chattering, but there was something about Ward—an intent way of listening—that made that so easy to do.

"Why does a young woman come back to a town with so few prospects?" he asked. "This morning Sophie suggested you had worked in New York."

She sighed. She had tried to give herself over to being carefree, but maybe it was impossible to be carefree when you carried burdens like she did.

She was already sorry she had confided so much, but she couldn't take it back, and it felt somehow good to share what was going on with the town, as if a burden she had carried silently was lightened. Why not go for broke? There was something about Ward that inspired confidences. And there was something in her, alone with all of this for so long, that she felt almost compelled to unburden. Maybe there was something about Ward being a near stranger, someone she would likely not see again, a safe person to share with.

"Kettle fell off his roof last year shoveling snow. I can't believe he was up there. He's in his sixties, for Pete's sake. He broke his hip. He needed help. Not that he asked for it."

"You gave up your aspirations to help him?"

"*Aspirations* might be a little grandiose. I was a clerk at a bank, baking a few scones on the side, which my friends were willing to pay for. But I came back to look after the Black Kettle. I'd worked my way up starting as a teenager there. I knew the ropes and no one else was available."

They walked silently for a while, and then he said, "So you were repaying a favor by coming back?"

"Not at all," she said quickly. "It's not a balance sheet. It's loving people. It's doing what needs to be done."

"Will you go back to your old life when Kettle is fully recovered?"

Sophie had already revealed her old life was a disaster, but she wasn't going to pursue that with a complete stranger. She had already talked way too much.

"This is my life now," Maddie said, determined and cheerful. "Kettle didn't have great medical coverage. I don't know how he's managing to keep the café open, but as long as he does, I'll help him in any way I can. We all have a great deal riding on the concert."

"You're so young to be carrying the worries of the world," he said softly. "Look, you're getting a little worry knot right here." He stopped and touched her forehead.

His finger pressed gently into her brow. She felt herself leaning into it. The weakness that overcame her was swift.

This was always her problem. When she most needed to be strong, she was not! But she would not fail herself this time.

Maddie stepped back from him and away from the odd comfort of the physical connection between them. "You caught me on a bad day," she said crisply. "I usually don't confide my life story to strangers."

"I'm glad you did. Sometimes, just to tell someone, can make your troubles seem smaller, aye?"

"Yes," she agreed, but grouchily. What would he know about it? This self-possessed man did not look as if he would have a problem in the world!

He regarded her thoughtfully. It seemed as if he could see her lonely nights, and her fret-filled days. Maddie had the uncomfortable feeling her heartbreak was an open book.

"Perhaps," he suggested, "you could leave them now? Your troubles. Just for this moment. Just for this beautiful spring afternoon. Here. Hang them on the branch of this tree."

It was silly. But also endearing. He took imaginary worries from around her neck, as if they were leis, his fingertips tickling briefly on that sensitive skin—touch number three—and hung them carefully on a low-hanging branch of the tree.

"You can pick them up again on your way out."

Ridiculously, she felt lighter! His casual contacts were making her feel as if she had been drinking champagne. But beneath the kind of tingling awareness of him, she felt wariness. He was very smooth. The kind of man who could make a woman believe in dreams again. And really, wasn't that the scariest thing of all?

"It's going to be okay," he said. "It always is."

He said this with utter confidence. Again, she felt the wariness of wanting to trust him. He was a man you could believe in. He was a man who could make you believe such a thing, even when the world, her world, had presented her with a great deal of evidence to the contrary.

But for this moment, with this powerful, self-assured man at her side in a forest that had stood strong for a thousand years, that had survived fires and storms and endless winters and the black hearts of greedy men, it felt as if maybe, just maybe she could believe it.

For one second, she put her wariness away and allowed herself to believe that everything would be okay.

CHAPTER SIX

WARD STOOD VERY STILL as Maddie searched his face, looking, he knew, for a truth she could hold on to. That everything would be all right.

She had no way of knowing that, as a prince, he often had the power and the resources to make everything right, and so when her shoulders dropped ever so slightly, and her forehead relaxed and a light came on in the deep green pools of her soulful eyes, he felt gratified.

She trusted *him*. Not the Prince of Havenhurst, but *him*. It was a first for him, to be trusted not for his influence and status—for what he could do for someone—but for something she saw in him. Ward felt some deep pleasure unfurl within him.

Of course, it was complicated. The very fact that she had no idea who he really was probably negated the heady trust he saw shining in her mossy eyes.

But he shook that off, and he took an imaginary necklace of worries from his own neck and hung it on the branch beside hers.

"You have worries?" she said.

"Aye, everyone has worries."

"And what are yours?"

It was a simple question. It occurred to him he had never confided his worries to anyone, except maybe ever so casually, every now and then, to Lancaster. What she was offering was different. And dangerous.

He backed swiftly away from the sanctuary he saw in

her eyes. They were strangers. He was going to enjoy a day of reprieve from his true identity. End of story.

He tapped the branch. "I've left them here. Today isn't a good day for worries of any kind. Perhaps when I pick them back up, I'll share them with you."

This, of course, was a lie. Still, hanging up his worries did not feel like a lie. It felt as if he had also hung up the remaining threads of who he was. Today, he was just an ordinary man. It felt like a gift.

For this brief moment in time—Prince Edward Alexander of Havenhurst—could be normal, experience normal, delight in normal. No one was watching his every move; the mantle of duty had been removed.

And he suspected Maddie needed *normal* as much as he did at this point in her life. Could they just be two ordinary people, enjoying each other, and these moments they had been given, before surrendering to the rigors and demands of the lives that would call them back?

They came to a part of the trail that narrowed, and they had to scramble over some rocks. Like an ordinary guy he went up first, and then he held out his hand to her. She hesitated, but then, her eyes never leaving his face, she took it.

Her hand felt small in his. And surprisingly strong. He helped her up over the rocks. She let go swiftly, as soon as the obstacles had been overcome.

Oddly, he missed the sensation of her hand in his. Perhaps because, as a prince, this was one of the things he had not experienced often: casual physical contact with other people, and particularly not pretty people!

To him, everything felt more intense than it had even moments previously. He drank it in with all the appreciation of a person who knew how relentlessly the clock ticked, as if he had been told he had days left to live.

They smelled the familiar earthy mineral smell of the pools before they arrived. Still, he was not prepared for the grotto when the forest opened up to it. It was breathtaking, like a mystical paradise. The growth was almost tropical, the steaming pools surrounded by lush greenness and ferns.

"It's like this even in the wintertime," Maddie told him. "The pools heat the air around them, allowing tropical plants to grow."

They had entered at the upper end by the highest of the three pools. Each pool was connected to the one beneath it by a small waterfall. The pools, where they were visible through thick shrouds of rising steam, were amazing colors, jade green and deep turquoise swirling into indigo blue.

"This top pool is the smallest and the hottest. Each pool gets progressively larger and cooler."

"And do you like it hot or cool, Miss Maddie?"

The words were out before he could stop them. Another first, an ordinary man flirting lightly with an ordinary girl. He had made her blush. But also, her eyes darkened with sudden and unexpected heat.

Stand down, he ordered himself. There was danger in uncharted territory. And that should not feel nearly as enticing as it did.

Maddie stared at Ward. What made a man so sure of himself? It was aggravating. That kind of confidence was just plain off-putting.

Or so she tried to tell herself, a flimsy defense against what she was feeling. Which was what?

Attraction.

"I prefer the water cool," she said primly.

And then she was annoyed with herself. It was a little harmless flirting! She had hung up her worries, and hopefully with them, that little voice that was constantly chiding and trying to see the future. Ward was here until tomorrow night after the concert. She didn't always have to be the serious one, she didn't always have to try and ferret out future disaster in a little harmless flirting and she did not have to live by the mantra *doom is imminent.*

"I like it hot," he said.

"Well, I'm going to start in the cool pool. It's not for the faint of heart. You do what you want."

He lifted an eyebrow at her. "Are you questioning my manliness?"

Good grief, no. "Yes," she said. And then added, "Bok-bok-bok."

"Are you calling me a chicken?" He looked so genuinely aggrieved that she found herself laughing.

She could just have fun. For once in her life she could just give herself over to having fun. She could listen to the voice of her father, suggesting she be bold.

"If that's a challenge, I'll beat you into the water."

"No, you won't." She took off running, unbuttoning her shirt as she went. She looked ahead, but could hear him pounding up the path behind her. She tried to struggle out of her shorts while still running. He caught up to her, but when he surged by her, she caught his shirt in her fist and nearly fell over as her shorts tangled around her legs. He pulled his shirt over his head and she found herself holding it. The broadness and utter male beauty of his naked back nearly made her lose her focus. But no, she stepped out of her shoes and shorts and raced after him. He stopped at the edge of the pool and sloughed off his own shorts and shoes.

For a moment, she froze, drinking in the sculpted perfection of his body, the broadness of his back and neck, the muscled strength of his naked thighs. She wasn't entirely sure those were swim trunks!

He froze, too, staring at her. And then he smiled ever so slightly. It occurred to Maddie he was hypnotizing her with his gorgeousness on purpose to win the challenge!

He broke her gaze and jumped.

"Oh, no you don't!" Maddie came out of her trance and made one final grab for him. Instead of evading her, he reached back and captured her hand and pulled her into the pool right after him.

The water was freezing! His hand felt as if it was sizzling where it was touching hers.

"I think I like it hot, after all," she said, breaking his grip, and thinking that his hot hand in the cold water was frighteningly sensual.

"Bok-bok-bok!"

"Oh!" She cupped her hands and sent a mighty splash into his face. "I'm not! Take that!"

"Be careful, Maddie," he said in warning. "You shouldn't start things you can't finish."

How true was that? Still, she couldn't resist splashing him again, this time swiping her whole forearm on the top of the water, sending a wave of the freezing water over top of him.

"Lion versus gazelle," he said wickedly, and reached for her.

Maddie glanced at the bank. There was no way she could get to it and scramble up it without him catching her.

He twirled an imaginary mustache and laughed villainously.

She threw herself away, swam with all her might, dived under the water and came up to find him right on her heels. She tried to back away, but she was laughing so hard she was choking on the mineral-laden water. She couldn't put much distance between them.

He splashed her with such force her nose filled up with water, and then while she was sputtering, swam away. But she quickly went after him, backed him against some rocks and unleashed a flurry of water at him. They went back and forth like that, filling the pools with the sounds of their shouting and laughter.

She recognized her defenses tumbling, one by one. She recognized she *needed* this, probably more than she knew. A giving over to playfulness, letting the lightness of her spirit rise to meet the lightness of his.

When the pool was too cold to stand a minute longer, they chased each other up the slope and jumped into the warmer one, and then into the one above that. Tired, and literally played out, they finally floated side by side in the hottest pool.

Finally, they found Sophie and Lancaster on a warm rock above the pools.

Lancaster was fully clothed. Sophie was sunning herself in a very skimpy bathing suit, while Lancaster pointedly ignored her.

"I'm glad someone is having fun," Sophie said snippily.

"You're not having fun?" Ward asked her.

"He didn't even get wet," Sophie sulked. "He seems to think he's the lifeguard."

Lancaster cast her a narrow-eyed glance, stood up and wordlessly left them. Moments later he was perched on a rock high above them that jutted out over the hottest pool. Somewhere along the way, he had lost most of his clothing.

Lancaster turned his back to them and spread his arms wide. It was obvious what he planned to do. The bravest— or the most reckless—of Mountain Bend boys sometimes jumped from that high outreach, but no one ever dived from it.

Like Ward, Lancaster seemed to be a man 100 percent positive of his own strength and his place in the world. He launched himself, backward, soaring up before starting to fall back toward the pool. He twisted in the air, arms tucked in close, legs straight, before slicing cleanly into the water. Moments later, he surfaced, shaking water droplets from his hair, laughing.

"He could have been killed," Sophie said, furious.

"Ah, that man could dive into a cup of water," Ward reassured her. "Where we come from we cut our teeth on this. In fact, I think I'll join him."

Soon, Ward was on the same perch Lancaster had been on earlier. Maddie suddenly understood Sophie's frightened fury. She had lived here all her life and never seen anyone dive into the pools like this. She, herself, had never even taken the terrifying jump from that place.

Ward turned his back to them, showing them the perfect curve of his spine, the broadness at the top of it and the slenderness at the bottom. He stood on his tiptoes and his calf muscles rippled.

Maddie wanted to object, too.

But the beauty of what unfolded stopped her. He launched himself backward, somersaulting one complete time before cutting cleanly into the water.

The men dived and dived and dived, each outdoing the other's previous dive.

Maddie was entranced, and she was pretty sure, despite all the shrieking, Sophie was as entranced as she was.

She felt as if they were doing the age-old dance—men showing women their strength and prowess, impressing them with it, making some hunger burn like a flame in their bellies. It had been a long time since she had been involved in this particular dance, and never really in this way. The men's strength was raw and easy, magnificent to behold.

Still, Maddie recognized her fascination was deeper than appreciation of the male form. It was with the boldness of it, the freedom and the faith one had to feel to throw themselves into the air like that, to trust the water would catch them.

Finally, as the light leached from the sky, the men stopped diving. They came and toweled off, laughter and power shimmering in the air around them.

"Can you teach me how to do that?" Maddie asked, when the men joined them. She was envious with how alive they seemed. She wanted, in that moment, as much as she had ever wanted anything, to taste the power and joy that shimmered in the air around them.

Don't be afraid to be bold.

But both men appeared very uncomfortable with her boldness. They regarded her silently.

"What?" Maddie demanded.

"It's too dangerous," Lancaster said.

"I'm afraid time has run out, anyway. Look at the light." Ward couldn't hide his relief, and Maddie couldn't help but feel he was protecting her, which made her feel quite nice, instead of properly outraged.

Besides, he was right. It was too dark now.

And maybe she was just a little relieved, too. What she had asked was scary. And besides, she already felt way too much attraction to Ward. Inviting further interaction might be more dangerous than the diving.

They sat on the blanket they had brought and ate the picnic that had been packed. It was nearly dark by the time they were done. The tension over her request dissipated, and Maddie and Ward talked lightly of the different interpretations of the sport of football, the worst food they had ever eaten and the best, their favorite music and movies. Sophie sulked silently as Lancaster sat slightly apart from them, aloof.

The night air was getting chilly, and Maddie was relieved that Sophie wasn't nearly as sophisticated as she wanted everybody to believe, not as desperate to get Lancaster's attention as Maddie had been concerned about. Like Maddie, she ducked behind a shrub to change back into dry clothes.

As they prepared to leave the grotto, Lancaster put himself in the lead.

"I should probably go first," Maddie said, "I know the way better."

Ward laughed, low in his throat.

"Women don't dive? Or lead the way?" Maddie asked, genuinely annoyed now. Somehow, after the light conversation earlier, the prickliness felt much safer.

"Humor me," Lancaster said, as if this was not even open to discussion. "I'll try not to lead you off any cliffs."

"I do not need two big strong guys to lead me through the woods!" Maddie said. "I grew up in these mountains."

"What if we meet a bear?" Lancaster asked her.

"How would you be better able to handle that than me?" Maddie challenged.

"I'm capable of tearing out his throat with my bare hands. Are you?"

For a moment they were all silent.

Maddie watched as Lancaster's eyes flicked to Ward. She remembered what Kettle had said, that he thought Lancaster was a close protection specialist. And hadn't Sophie noticed something, too? *He thinks he's the lifeguard.* And at supper, sitting apart from them, not engaging with them. She tried to think. Had he been watchful?

Something shivered along Maddie's awareness. These men really were not who they said they were.

What did they say they're doing here? Kettle had asked.

Maddie gave herself a little shake and acquiesced to Lancaster's desire to be in the lead. None of it mattered. Tomorrow her life would be back to normal. *Normal* had become a highly overrated experience. There was no need to read deep dark secrets into this. The men obviously came from a more traditional culture. There was no sense trying to fix that, or change it, in this one-off encounter with them.

In the darkness, she could see Ward watching her. He smiled and when she stumbled over a root on the dark path and nearly fell, he reached for her hand and steadied her.

Just as well, then, she wasn't in the lead. She could feel the quiet strength in him. His ingrained instinct to protect her. Maybe a man's traditional need to lead and protect wasn't such a bad thing! Maddie took a deep breath and squeezed Ward's hand and then let it go before it felt too nice to hold it.

Still, she recognized, once again, she was being way too serious, and she didn't want to spoil what remained of this experience.

Even in the dark, they both recognized the branch of the tree where they had hung their worries. They paused and looked at the branch, and then at each other.

Without saying a word, they both moved by it, and the laughter blossomed naturally between them.

"I do not see anything funny," Sophie said, obviously in a very poor humor indeed.

They finally stumbled through the darkness to the car. Ward drove down the tricky mountain road in the dark, and asked directions to Maddie's house. He stopped in front.

"Is this one of the original miner's cottages you talked about earlier?"

She nodded, flattered that he listened so carefully, and she turned and looked at her house through his eyes. Her home was tiny, but adorable, with its yellow painted front porch and shutters and its deep mauve siding. Flower boxes bloomed cheerfully under the windows. The houses on either side of it were not quite so well loved. One had a For Sale sign that had been hanging so long one of its hooks had rotted away, and it hung crookedly.

"I live just down the street. I'll get out here, too," Sophie said. Lancaster got out and opened her door for her. She tossed her hair and marched by him with her nose in the air. He raised a brow at Maddie and shrugged.

Ward stood looking down at Maddie. Her heart began to pound. Did he feel the same as her? That there would only be one magical way that would be suitable to end such a magical day?

He took a step back from her.

She took a step back from him.

"Will you be at the concert?" he asked, finally, breaking the silence between them.

"I don't have a ticket." She didn't want to admit that she had refused a free ticket from Sophie, whose cousin had supplied her with several. The other tickets had been priced right out of her range. She had realized she had become the person who always said no instead of yes. She had said no to a free concert ticket to the Ritz, preferring to stay in the safety of her home, with her book and her bath, where she controlled everything, where nothing surprising ever happened.

"I'll find you a ticket," he said. "Please come with me."

"I have to think about it," Maddie stammered. Yes, she did. She had to think. She had to think carefully. She had such a powerful attraction to this man. Why torment herself, getting in deeper, when it could not go anywhere?

Not that she wanted things to go anywhere! She had learned her lessons!

"I wouldn't go to the concert with you if you were the last man on earth," Sophie shouted over her shoulder at Lancaster.

"I hate to break it to you, lass, but you weren't asked," Lancaster called after her.

"Sparks," Ward noted, his eyes unrelenting on her own turned-up face.

"Fire danger high," Maddie returned huskily.

And then they stared at each other. Because it seemed as if they could be talking about Sophie and Lancaster.

But they both knew they weren't.

Which was all the more reason to say no.

She willed herself to say no. She had to say no. What was going to happen after the concert when he left for good? She would have had this little taste of excitement, that little tingle of anticipation, that tiny expectation of something out of the ordinary happening. And when that was gone? Wouldn't life seem like it was without light? Without meaning? Without hope?

Had her life become like that? And if it had, wasn't it up to her to fix it? Wasn't that the whole lesson of Derek? *You are responsible for your own life. Your own happiness. Do not count on other people. Particularly handsome, charming, make-you-weak-in-the-knees people.*

Say no! It was going to be worse if she allowed their lives to tangle for yet one more day. So the sensible answer to his invitation was no. The only answer.

But she could not say it.

Why not, just this once, allow life to surprise her? Why not see where it all went? If it went nowhere at all, she would have had a great night at an outdoor concert. Surely, that had to be preferable to sitting at home?

"If you find a ticket," she said.

But she would probably find herself sitting at home, regardless. The tickets had been sold out for weeks. He wasn't going to find one. Or was he? He looked like the kind of man who pulled the impossible out of thin air routinely.

Ward grinned at her, as if he had a ticket already!

CHAPTER SEVEN

MADDIE HAD THOUGHT Ward would show up at the Black Kettle sometime during the day, at least to tell her they had not been successful in getting the ticket. But he did not. She was aware that, despite the fact she had been telling herself all day it was better if she didn't go, as each hour passed she was more disappointed.

Not that there was much time for any kind of introspection: the Black Kettle was absolutely packed all day long.

Then just before closing, an envelope was delivered to her by a courier. A courier in Mountain Bend! It held a single ticket to the concert, and a note.

I'll pick you up. Eight o'clock.

Just before Ward arrived to pick her up, Maddie had an attack of nerves so bad, she thought she wouldn't be able to go to the concert. He was leaving, for heaven's sake. This was not going anywhere. He didn't even live in the same country.

Her head knew all of that. But when she touched the pendant on her neck, Maddie was intensely aware her heart was singing a different tune. Her heart was telling her she had not felt so alive, ever.

Not even the initial excitement of New York had made her feel like this. Not Derek. Not the thought of starting her own baking business. Nothing.

She realized part of her had been shut down since the

second blow to her life: her mother leaving her, just as her father had. But no, that wasn't it. Not precisely. After the death of her mother, there had been a wild time when she was grief stricken, looking for release from all that pain, looking for love...

Pregnant. She had a pregnancy scare by some beautiful boy who had made her heart do *exactly* what Ward was doing to it now. That boy hadn't even known her name.

She remembered those terrifying days of being so alone with the shame and guilt and remorse, playing out her whole frightening future as a single mom, wondering how she could live with the disappointment of everyone who expected her to be the sensible one.

It had turned out to be a false alarm. But she had never really trusted herself since then, as if she, and she alone, knew there was a wild girl inside of her who simply could not be trusted when a certain man looked at her a certain way.

Derek had not been that man. Had she chosen him precisely because he did not make her lose that precious control? Had he sensed something in her holding back? Was that why he had turned to her friend?

But Ward made her feel that way: on fire with life, reckless.

If he had given her a cell phone number, she would call him now and plead illness. But he had not.

Maddie went and looked at herself in the mirror. She had deliberately chosen an outfit that was conservative, not in any way sexy. She wore jeans, and a T-shirt; she had put a casual blazer over the top because spring nights in the mountains were notoriously cool.

It was an outfit that said she was a decent girl who did not chase strange men around hot pools. An outfit that said, *I know you're leaving, I don't have to impress you. I won't do anything I'll regret.*

But despite the conservative, if contrived, *I don't care* look, she saw something in her eyes that made her a different woman than she had been yesterday morning.

Really, she looked as though she had been kissed! If she looked like this after an innocent afternoon of chasing around the pools, what was she going to look like—be like—when he did kiss her?

Was he going to kiss her?

Of course he was going to kiss her! She had seen it in his eyes as surely as she was feeling it stirring in her own soul. Passion. Hunger. And then he was going to leave, she reminded herself. He might even promise to stay in touch, but he wouldn't. They lived in different worlds.

In other words, she had nothing to lose. She didn't have to care what kind of impression she made on him. She didn't have to be the sensible one. It was a one-night thing.

In light of her dawning realization of complete freedom, the outfit suddenly felt all wrong. Feeling emboldened, Maddie went and changed clothes.

She had a dress that she had always worn over tights. It was a sleeveless shimmering aquamarine with a band of embroidery embellishing the deep V of the neck. It was extremely short, but wearing it as a dress instead of a top made her feel fun and flirty and bold and daring.

"I have great legs!" she told herself, twirling in front of the mirror. She burst out laughing and hugged herself. How long since she had felt exhilaration like this?

She was the wallflower who had been unexpectedly invited to the prom, and she wanted to make the most of her moment. She was ready to be seen differently. She felt young and excited. She felt as if—for the first time in a long time, or maybe even the first time ever—she wanted to be memorable. She wanted to be sexy.

Ward was going to leave. But that didn't mean she couldn't be a brand-new person! In fact, it gave her the complete liberty to be a brand-new person!

The doorbell rang. Maddie's confidence fled.

Don't answer it, she begged herself. But that other part of her ran her fingers through her curls, so they sprang even more wildly about her head, and that other part of her put a dab of lip gloss on, and that other part of her sprayed perfume in the air and then walked through it.

She touched the pendant, hoping for some sensible advice. Instead, she remembered how wildly her father had loved her mother, how impetuously. Her father used to sing to her mother, his arms wrapped around her waist, his chin resting on her shoulder.

Good grief! She was going to a concert! Maddie went and opened the door.

We should have picked up those worries, she thought. Worries kept people sensible.

The way Ward looked did not make her feel sensible. He was wearing dark glasses, which he removed to look at her. Whiskers had darkened his face; his eyes were as navy blue as midnight. He wore jeans, the dark denim creased and very navy blue, like his eyes. They clung to the large muscles of his thighs. He had on a button-down casual shirt and a leather jacket. He was wearing a dark fedora, which one in a million men might be able pull off. He was that one man. He looked like he could model for the cover of *GQ*!

Despite her effort at being conservative, his gaze took her in and was loaded with a subtle male appreciation that left her feeling breathless.

Charmingly, he handed her the cutest little posy of

wildflowers and she buried her nose in it, so he wouldn't see what was in her eyes, which was sure to be longing. For his strength, and his closeness, and his lips, and the scrape of those whiskers across the tender skin of her face.

He was a stranger. She didn't think it would be a good idea to let this newfound sense of liberty get out of hand.

Her eyes drifted over Ward's shoulder, and she saw Lancaster waited at the vehicle. *Lancaster*, she thought with relief. *Chaperone.*

But then, for a chaperoned lady, she had the wildest thought. *We're going to kiss good-night. When he brings me home, should I invite him in for a hot chocolate? A glass of wine? Could that be misinterpreted? Could she trust herself, in the privacy of her own home, not to want to taste him, touch him?*

Maddie took a jacket from the coat closet. Thankfully, spring nights in the mountains could be chilly and the coat covered most of the outfit she now realized was way too skimpy.

CHAPTER EIGHT

THE ATMOSPHERE AT the concert was electric. Though the outdoor amphitheater had bleachers built into the hills that surrounded the stage area, everyone was standing. The band came out, and from the first note it was obvious the acoustics were going to be unbelievable. The crowd went wild. There was no warm-up time. In seconds, everyone was dancing and singing along.

Maddie felt something in her let loose, some inhibition she had carried her whole life—except for one regrettable moment when she had paid dearly for it—let go. This time, she told herself, she was safe. This time, there would be no price to pay for just being herself.

Within minutes, she had the jacket off. The music was so loud it felt as if it was inside of her. She had the best time. She danced with Ward. She danced with strangers— aware she was still dancing for Ward. Then she danced with Ward again. She had never felt quite so confident, so on fire with life.

Only Lancaster seemed immune to the music and the energy, tense and grim. At the intermission they—or, more accurately, Lancaster—pushed their way through the crowds, and they found the refreshment booth.

As they waited in line, a whisper began to go through the crowd.

"A prince? Where? That's ridiculous."

Maddie glanced around. She didn't see anything or anybody who looked like a prince. She noticed that Ward, who had taken off his dark glasses, took them out of his jacket pocket and slid them back on.

"It's him, I tell you. I saw a pic of him on Entertainment World. *He was at Sea O'Brian's villa in California."*

"Yes, you're right. I remember..."

Maddie was craning her neck like everyone else to see what was going on. But then she noticed Lancaster and a shiver went up and down her spine. He looked grim. Every muscle in his body was tensed, as if for battle. His hand was resting ever so lightly on his hip. Her eyes widened as she saw there was a bulge there. Was Lancaster carrying a weapon? But why?

And why had Ward put those glasses back on? It was dark out.

"Move," he breathed tersely in her ear. Lancaster went into action with such swiftness that it was stunning. He blocked Ward's body, and hers, with his own. He plowed through the crowd, like a ship cutting a wake that she and Ward walked in. The crowd parted without protest in front of his formidable form. Ward's hand found hers, but there was nothing romantic about it. There was urgency in his touch.

"What is going on?"

"Follow Lancaster," he ordered her sternly. "No questions. Not right now."

"It is him," somebody screamed, holding up a picture on their phone for all to see. "It's Prince Edward of Havenhurst."

Suddenly, it seemed everyone had a phone out. And all of them were aimed at Ward. People were gaping at him. Women looked starstruck. People were starting to shout his name. Maddie wanted to laugh. It was an error, obviously, a bad case of mistaken identity. Maybe the desire to laugh was a form of hysteria—it felt as if her world was tilting crazily.

Except she could tell from the sudden closed look on Ward's face it was not a mistake. She could tell from the way Lancaster had gone into battle mode.

Lancaster, the close protection specialist, was parting the crowds with a look. He had not yet had to use physical force; his warrior countenance was enough.

Prince?

She felt something catch in her throat, as they pushed through the crowds. Why the pretense? Why hadn't he told her?

She slipped her hand out of his.

"I can explain," he said.

Hadn't she heard that before? Hadn't that been Derek's exact phrase when she'd found him with her best friend when she'd decided to surprise him by coming to New York for the weekend?

The answers were coming from the rising swell in the crowd around her.

"A real prince?"

"I'm Googling it—yes, a real prince!"

"Havenhurst. It's in the North Atlantic."

"Edward Alexander the Fourth."

Everyone who was not taking pictures on their phones seemed to be looking up facts about Havenhurst and its Prince.

Pieces seemed to fall into place with stunning clarity for Maddie: she had *known* these men weren't who they said they were. Kettle had actually told her Lancaster was a bodyguard! So there had been plenty of moments when she could have come to her senses and what had she done?

She had pooh-poohed her own instincts. She had chosen to believe in fairy tales—ironic since it appeared Ward was a prince!

No wonder, at the pools, Lancaster had remained aloof to the playful atmosphere. Sophie would be happy to know it had nothing to do with her! He'd been at work. He had not relaxed until Ward was out of the pools. Even then, he had undressed away from them. Probably because he was concealing that very weapon his hand was resting close to now! When Ward decided to follow his lead and dive, Lancaster dived with him. Not showing off at all. Doing his job. Taking the lead that dark night out of the pools, because it was his job, if a bear materialized, to put his body between it and his Prince.

Now Lancaster had a look of fierce determination on his face, searching for a way to get Ward out of the crush of a crowd that now knew he was no ordinary man.

Lancaster shoved Ward toward a temporary security fence that had been erected around the concert area. He had seen a door concealed in it that Maddie had not seen. It opened under a shove from his shoulder, and he stood, his back braced against it as Maddie and Ward passed through. Lancaster stood for a moment, eyeing the crowd—daring them—and then he turned and went out the door and closed it behind himself. He found a piece of rock and wedged it under the jamb.

It seemed suddenly very dark and very silent. But it lasted only seconds. Another door in the fence, several yards down, opened and people began to spill out.

The Google-fueled chatter started again.

"He's engaged."

Maddie felt something in her freeze.

"To a real princess."

"It's like a fairy tale."

But for Maddie, it was not like a fairy tale, at all, but like the return of a familiar nightmare.

Lancaster put his arm around Ward's shoulder and they bolted toward the parking lot. Ward reached for her hand, but she evaded his grasp. The crowd surged by her in hot pursuit of his celebrity.

Now she turned quickly and pushed her way against the crowds.

She heard her name called, once, desperately.

"Maddie!" It was Ward. No, *Edward*.

She turned and walked backward. She did something she had never done, in her entire life.

She presented Edward Alexander the Fourth, Prince of Havenhurst, engaged to a real live princess, with her middle finger.

With some satisfaction, she registered the distress on his face and the shock on Lancaster's. Apparently, it wasn't protocol to present the Prince with your middle finger!

She walked home, taking a well-known trail through the forest, feeling sick to her stomach, remembering *everything*. He had teased her about her name that first day at work. She had thought he was flirting with her. But no, he was accustomed to people being uncomfortable with his status. He was used to putting people who were intimidated by him at ease. From teasing her about a Celt being in the kitchen, to complimenting her scones and tea, it was all part of that graciousness of being born to an elevated position in life.

No wonder he was so good at listening intently. No wonder he was so sure of himself.

They weren't from Scotland. That's why he'd hesitated when she asked if there were Boy Scouts in Scotland.

As she walked home, Maddie was aware of a change in herself.

She didn't feel victimized. She didn't feel sad. She didn't feel as if she was going to break down and cry.

No, she felt as angry as she had ever felt in her entire life.

Ward watched helplessly as the waves and waves of people separated him from Maddie. He could see the fury in the set of her shoulders and the stiffness of her spine.

He had to get to her.

"Let her go," Lancaster said roughly when he saw Ward's intent. "The mob was so focused on you they didn't figure out she was with you. It won't do her any good if they do."

He was right, plus Maddie was moving swiftly, putting more and more people between him and her with every determined footstep that she took. It was obvious there would be no getting to her now.

They got to the car and Lancaster shoved him in unceremoniously, got in the driver's seat, and they left the crowd behind them.

"That was one of the worst moments of my life," Lancaster said, after a moment.

No lecture, of course, though Lancaster had been adamant the whole trip in general, and the concert in particular, had the potential to become security nightmares.

Ward thought of Maddie's stricken look when she first realized the depth of his lie to her. He looked out the window. He had betrayed her trust, something he was sure, given Sophie's revelations that day in the café, that she did not give easily.

"And mine," he said softly, "and mine."

"Do you want me to find her?"

"Of course."

"Let's just find a different car, first. This one is highly recognizable." But for all Lancaster's amazing skill, this time it was not enough. Though they patrolled every street of Mountain Bend, and drove by her house several times, they did not see Maddie Nelson.

Ward's phone buzzed in his pocket. Unreasonably, he hoped it was Maddie, though he knew he had not given her the number.

But it wasn't Maddie. It was Sea O'Brian.

Telling him, breathless with excitement, that she had to cancel her engagement to him. She'd been offered the lead role in an upcoming television series. Which could give her flagging career a better shot in the arm? Playing princess on some remote island, or taking the role?

She had taken the role.

Ward slipped his phone back into his pocket.

Lancaster cast him a glance. "Sir? Everything all right?"

Wearily, Ward explained what had just happened. The silence stretched between them as they drove every street in Mountain Bend looking for Maddie.

Finally, one last drive past her house, the lights were on, and Ward saw a shadow move on one of the closed drapes of the front window. He felt both relief that she had made it home safely, and trepidation that he had to talk to her. He had to set things straight. Though, so far, his efforts to make things right with women were not unfolding all that well.

"I'm going in," he said.

"Sir, we know she's safe. She seemed, er, a little angry when we left her. Maybe a cooling-off period is in order?"

A little angry might be the understatement of the century. Ward was certain he had never seen a woman an-

grier than Maddie had just been, walking, backward, away
from him, making a gesture that represented all of her
barely restrained fury.

He didn't want a cooling-off period. He wanted to
tackle this right now. He was astonished by the fact he felt
faintly thrilled when he considered confronting that fury.

He opened the door of the car and stepped out.

CHAPTER NINE

"Go away," Maddie called in the direction of her front door.

Ward's arrival was nothing like the ones in fairy tales. He hadn't ridden up on a white charger; there were no trumpets blowing. If he pounded her door much harder, it was going to break loose from the frame!

She had been home over an hour. She was in her pajamas, sipping tea and looking at a book, though she found herself unable to comprehend the words. For once in her life, the book was not providing the escape she had always looked to books for. Even in the most difficult circumstances a book could carry her away. But not tonight.

She was in her nicest pajamas having tea out of her good china. The book had been chosen to make her look sophisticated in her reading material. All of that probably meant she had both expected his arrival and intended to let him in. Sooner or later.

"Maddie, please talk to me."

"Is that a royal decree?" Still, she could feel the weakness, as it had been from the first time he had pleaded with her to go to the hot pools with him.

Please say yes. Please come with me. There was something about the way Ward said *please* that disarmed her, that had disarmed her from the beginning, that had made her say yes to taking him to the hot pools and yes to the concert, when she should have been saying no.

She should have been protecting herself against this

very thing that was now unfolding. Unwanted drama in her life. Uncalled-for complications. Betrayals and lies.

The weakness could be lack of food, Maddie told herself. She'd been too excited before the concert to eat, and now, even though she was hungry, food did not appeal.

The pounding came on the door again. She would not have him thinking she was hiding. That she was cowering behind her door, afraid of him, or crying her heart out.

And so she got up deliberately, set down her teacup and her book. She must have got up too quickly because she felt woozy. She took a breath, steadied herself and went to the door. She threw it open, and then folded her arms across her chest and planted her legs firmly, determined not to let him see she actually felt both emotionally and physically weak at the moment.

His arm, raised to bash her door again, fell to his side. It was really unfair that he looked so charming. Since he was a prince. And since this wasn't any kind of a fairy tale with a happily-ever-after in the script.

Okay, so he looked very tired. And slightly disheveled in a very unprincely way. In a way that made her want to run her fingers through his mussed hair and smooth it back into place, as if he, somehow, was the one in need of sympathy here!

Buck up, Maddie told herself. Ward had deliberately withheld information about himself. He had pretended to be someone he was not. He had been toying with her when he was engaged to someone else.

"Unconscionable," Maddie greeted him without preamble.

"I agree," he said.

Maddie did not want him to be agreeable! She didn't want to look at him; she didn't want to fall into the pools of his eyes one more time. So she looked past him. Over his shoulder, she saw the "normal" guy persona had been abandoned. The Lambo was gone, replaced with something black, shiny, solid.

Probably bulletproof.

"What do you want?" she demanded, hardening her heart to the look on his face, the intensity of the way he looked at her, the almost-electrical ripple it caused to surge inside of her.

"To explain."

"What's to explain? You lied to me. You did it deliberately and you did it often. You didn't tell me who you really were, and you were flirting with me while you were engaged to someone else! Scout's honor?"

"You have a right to be angry."

"Thank you, Your Royal Princeship. Are you giving me permission to feel mad? Mad as in Maddie? Should I curtsy now?" She glared at him. "Are you smiling?"

"I'm trying not to. It's just that—"

"Just that what?"

"No one has ever spoken to me that way. Not in my whole life."

"Being given the finger must have been a novelty for you, then, too."

"Indeed it was."

"If you start laughing, I'll kill you." Did she actually feel something softening toward him? No, she simply wasn't feeling well. *Buck up*, she reminded herself.

"Lancaster won't allow it. My killing."

"Yes, I've figured out Mr. Lancaster's role in things."

"Major, actually."

"Well, Major Lancaster is a long way away, Prince Whatever-your-real-name-is." She squinted through the darkness at where Lancaster waited, arms folded across his chest, rear rested against the door of the car, looking up and down the street. Watching. "He's looking the wrong direction for the danger. It's right in front of you."

"Indeed it is," he said, and even though his tone was solemn, his lips twitched.

"Oh!" she said, and stepped back from the door. "Come in. Let's get it over with."

He stepped over the threshold. Pure power rode into her tiny cottage with him. She wondered how humble it looked through his eyes. She decided she didn't care.

She gestured at the sofa. "Sit. Spit it out. I'm not offering tea."

He took the sofa. She stood across from him, arms still folded. But he had an air of command about him, and she knew he wouldn't say what he had to say until she sat down. With a sigh of long-suffering she flounced onto the chair across from him, picked up her now-cold tea and took a long sip, just to reinforce she was not offering him one.

"First, let me tell you why I didn't reveal my identity," he said, quietly.

She actually wanted to hear about the *real* Princess first, but she bit her tongue. Why appear like a jealous shrew? He had never promised her anything. The fact that he was here possibly meant he had a shred of integrity, though, really? She did not feel inclined to give him the benefit of the doubt.

All the playfulness was gone from him. "Havenhurst is my life. It's a very tiny island kingdom in the North Atlantic, with a Celtic culture. We have a population of about a million people. My duty is to those people. That duty comes before everything.

"Our main industries, in the past, have been logging and mining. Those are, as you know, limited resources. They both were managed poorly and petered out, leaving the island economically depressed and in a desperate situation."

Despite herself, Maddie found she was interested. This *was* like Mountain Bend. She needed to know if the story was going to have a happy ending.

"People were leaving the island in hope of work elsewhere. It was a truly grim situation. The island was now losing its most valuable resource—people. It was becoming a place of ghosts."

Again, the very same future Mountain Bend was facing. Despite herself, she could feel herself leaning toward him, interested. "What happened?"

"We have an abundance of hot springs on the island, so we are slowly reviving our economy with tourism and export of some of our mineral waters, which claim health benefits. I have taken on the economy as my main responsibility. But I have others. One is an expectation of a marriage that will bring benefit to our island. And that's part of what brought me to America.

"I wanted to sample normal. That's why I didn't tell you who I was."

Maddie grudgingly accepted that explanation. She could see that a man might not want to print *Prince* on his business card, that he might want to be liked for himself, but the engagement part?

"I'm supposed to be married soon."

His announcement was joyless.

"Yes, I couldn't help but hear that from the googling throngs."

"Yes, but you heard it was Aida. The other part of my trip here is that I came to ask someone else to marry me. Have you heard of Sea O'Brian?"

"The actress?"

"Yes."

It was a stark reminder of the rarified circles he moved in. It was a stark reminder of yet more treachery!

"Are you telling me you have two fiancées?" Maddie breathed.

"Um—"

"You cad! You've been flirting with me for two days!"

He was smiling again.

"Stop it! I'm dead serious."

"I know. But as I say, I've never been shrieked at before. It's, er, refreshing."

"Shrieked?" she inquired dangerously. "I did not shriek."

"I'm sorry. Let me think of another way to put it." He was silent for an insultingly long time. "Squealed at?"

"Oh!"

He frowned. "Yelped at?"

"I think you have to leave now."

"Just a few more moments of your time."

"Humph. This had better be good."

"Marriages, in my family, and on my island are not love matches, Maddie. It was decided when I was a child that one day I would marry Princess Aida Montego of the island that neighbors ours. Wynfield is our biggest ally and trading partner. This isn't a choice. It's a business decision, made by our fathers. Contracts were signed a very long time ago."

"But what about love?" she asked, aghast despite herself. "Oh!" she clapped her hand over her mouth. "That's where Sea O'Brian comes in, isn't it? You love her."

No reason to feel sad! The man was a cad.

"No," he said, "I don't love her. And she's just told me no, in any case."

She ordered herself not to feel relieved. That made him a worse cad, didn't it?

"Though," he continued, "to be sure, love plays a part in this story, but not Sea's part. Aida met a young man. She loves him madly. And he her. She would still do what is expected of her. She would marry me, even as she loves another. She really would have no choice, and we were both raised with the notion we were not to expect personal happiness."

"Not to expect personal happiness?" Maddie asked. On the other hand, maybe it was a good thing. The pursuit of happiness could lead to very poor decisions, as she well knew. Maybe his family was onto something!

"When you are born into a royal family," Ward said, "it is drummed into you from birth—service before self."

"I don't know what to say. Despite the fact I can see the practicality of it—an expectation of happiness can cause no end of problems, after all—I'm appalled for you, and I'm appalled for that poor girl."

"If I returned from America married," Ward said softly, "then she would be free. One of us, at least, could have some chance at personal happiness."

Maddie's mouth fell open.

"I reached an agreement with Sea to play the role of my wife," he said. "To set Aida free. Now, unfortunately, Sea has been made a better offer, and I am back at square one."

Despite herself, Maddie found the story—and his honor, his interest in giving Aida a life he had not asked or expected for himself—brought tears to her eyes. She saw in front of her a man who had everything: title, wealth, power. And yet he had no expectation of the greatest richness of them all, love.

"But now what?" she asked him, her anger completely gone.

"I'm not sure."

"People cannot be forced to marry one another in this day and age. It's archaic."

"Ah, yes. *Archaic.* That is probably as good a word as any to describe Havenhurst."

"You have to get out of this," Maddie said vehemently, "Not just to save Aida, but to save yourself."

"I agree. But I don't know anyone else who would be willing to return to Havenhurst as my wife. I'd have to know something of their character." He paused. He frowned. He stared at her. "Unless—"

He was looking at her so intently, her heart began to pound. She wiped her sweating palms on her pajamas.

"What?" she stammered.

"What if my meeting you was not mere coincidence, but chance meeting opportunity? What if it was whatever people called these stunning moments in time when the seemingly absurd, the impossible, manifests into destiny?"

Maddie stared at him. She felt light-headed. She really should have had some crackers with her tea.

"What are you saying?" she whispered.

He cocked his head at her. That smile tickled the gorgeous sensuous curve of his bottom lip.

"I'm asking you if you would consider being my wife."

CHAPTER TEN

WARD WATCHED AS Maddie tried to absorb what he had just said. He didn't blame her. He was stunned that he had said it himself. He watched the blood drain from her face. She reached for her tea, as though a sip would steady her, but her hand was shaking.

And then the teacup slid from her hand, spilling tea all over her and landing on the floor with a clatter. He leaped to his feet, afraid she had burned herself.

But before he could close the distance between them, her eyes got a glazed look in them, rolled back in her head, and she went completely limp, as though there were not a bone in her entire body. He reached her, just as her body crumpled from her chair.

Ward slid his hands under her and caught her before she hit the floor. He cradled her, one arm at the bend in her knees, the other around her shoulders.

"Maddie?" he called softly. Her eyes fluttered, but didn't open. He hefted her against his chest and took the seat she had been on, feeling her warmth seep into him.

He looked down into her face. How had she become so familiar in such a short period of time? The faint freckles, the scattering of hair, the delicacy of feature?

Maddie looked so pale and so frail. It was as if her every vulnerability was open to him. Why had he done this to her? Why had he invited her to participate in a deception? It was all wrong, and she was the wrong person for it.

Still, it was done. He had asked. She was sensible. She would say no.

He thought he should get a damp cloth, or call Lancaster, who was more adept at first aid than he was, but instead, he did something he was not sure he had ever done.

Except maybe once, when he had decided not to marry Aida.

He listened to his heart, and he dropped his lips to the smoothness of her brow.

Her eyes fluttered open.

And at first, she smiled, as if she had been having the best of dreams.

But then, she struggled against him. "What on earth?"

"You fainted. Shush, don't struggle like that. Just relax for a moment. Regain yourself."

She followed the instruction in that she quit struggling, but she was stiff in his arms, a frown on her face as she gazed up at him.

"I did not faint," she decided. "I'm not the fainting type."

"Well, I did not poison your tea, so unless you have another theory?"

Her frown deepened. She rubbed at her forehead. "Did you kiss me?"

He decided silence might be the best defense!

"Oh," she said, brightening. "I get it. It's a dream. Kissed by a prince and all that rot."

"I think the rot part might be a little strong," he said, pretending insult.

"So, it's not a dream. I have a real live prince in my house. Don't get the idea I swooned for you. I haven't eaten properly today," she said defensively.

"It had nothing to do with me asking you to marry me?"

Her eyes went very round. "Nothing," she whispered.

"A business arrangement," he said softly.

Did she look disappointed? Had he led her to believe something else? That it would be real?

Would she have gone for that?

Ward realized he could not allow himself to think of that: of Maddie forever his. Of waking in the mornings to those green eyes and that small smile, of being treated like a normal man. Of being told to go sod himself when that was what he needed to hear. Of chasing each other, the way they had chased through the hot pools.

Of possessing her in every way a man possessed his wife.

No, he could not go there. This woman, who had suffered so many losses—parents, fiancé, career—deserved something he could not give her.

A family. A normal, wholesome all-American family.

But what he could give her, a tender gift to her, was a way out of the challenges she was facing now. He was in a position to make sure the benefits of marrying him outweighed her reservations and overcame her anger.

"A business arrangement," she said, her tone wooden.

"I can make it worth your while, Maddie, well worth your while."

"I can't."

"Why?"

"It's just wrong. It's deceitful, for one thing. For another, think of the poor example it sets for someone like Sophie. You marry a man you just met? Because he's a prince? Because he can solve your problems and give you things?"

He decided now would probably not be the safest time to tell her that her voice had become a little shrill again.

"I think you should give it some thought."

She seemed to realize she was still in his arms. This

time, when she struggled, he let her go. She found her feet, a trifle unsteadily, but still folded her arms over her chest and planted her legs apart, a posture intended to show strength even if she still looked pale and shaky.

"I'll do no such thing," she said.

"It's more than evident the whole town is struggling, including the Black Kettle."

"And?"

"Please sit down before you go down again. Maddie, I can help. I can show you some of our mineral water exports. Not to mention what your newfound notoriety could do for tourism. Mountain Bend, home of an American princess."

He found he could not take his eyes off her. She was adorably cute when she was fuming like that. Had he thought this through properly? Wasn't the cute factor going to make the arrangement he had just suggested more complicated?

Maybe not. She had called him a liar. A cad. And a sneak. She had called his kisses "rot." Another man, a saner man, might be withdrawing his offer and heading for the door.

But he did not feel sane. Not at all.

He felt as if he was a man who had waited his whole life for this moment: honesty. Someone who was strong enough to be completely straightforward with him. Funny, that honor would come wrapped in such a fragile-looking little package. He suspected Maddie was hiding strength she did not even know about.

"I thought the concert would save him," she said, her voice hollow, "and help Mountain Bend."

"I think it's a case of too little, too late. No business can be saved on the strength of one night's success. You would need to look at becoming a regular concert venue.

Which is a possibility. I could have my business team look into it."

Maddie looked stricken. He could see tears behind her eyes. Her loyalty and her ability to love, coupled with that honesty, made her both a good choice, and a very, very complicated one for him.

But the choice was not his alone. He had given her the facts, as he knew them. Now he had to trust her to make the decision that would be best for her.

He hoped it would also be the one that was best for him.

"I didn't tell you my assessment of the town to make you feel threatened," he said. He closed the distance between them and caught a tear as it slid down her cheek.

She slapped his hand away and moved back from him. She rubbed furiously at her eyes.

"Really? I'll be out of a job soon, Sophie's college dreams will be up in smoke and Kettle will be out on the street, and you didn't intend for me to feel threatened?"

"I didn't create any of that situation," he pointed out. "I'm offering a way out of it. But the choice is yours. Marry me. Be my wife for one year, three hundred and sixty-five days. I'll come back in the morning. You can let me know your final decision."

She looked as if she planned to let him know her final decision right now! And in the shrill voice, too.

But then she stopped herself. She just looked tired and pale and Ward thought the decent thing to do would be to say he would look after things no matter what she decided.

But something stopped him from saying that, too.

They both needed time to think, obviously.

"Come back early," she said. "Before I start work."

"All right." If she said no, she would just go to work as if it was an ordinary day. Even though she knew what the future held. There was a kind of bravery in that, he supposed.

He realized he did not want her to say no and that there was bravery in saying yes, too.

"Can I help you?" he asked. "Get to bed?"

Her eyes widened as if he had propositioned her. Ward realized seeing her bedroom might not be a good idea.

"Get something to eat?" he said hastily.

"No." Her voice was proud. "Please, go."

"Can I call Sophie to come be with you?"

"Please, just go."

He took one more look at her face, and then went and quietly let himself out the door. He had an unusual moment of self-doubt. What had he just done? He had held out a carrot to her, that given her love and loyalty, he did not think she was going to be able to refuse.

This was how he'd been raised: get what you want. Use whatever means it takes to get it. He had borne witness to his father's ability to be ruthless on many, many occasions.

Was he just like him?

No, because his father would be gleeful at the kind of predicament he had just put Maddie in.

She would have trouble saying no.

But Ward didn't feel gleeful. Not at all. He felt like the cad she had accused him of being.

So he would save Aida. And he would save himself from marriage, an institution he did not think he had any capacity for, given what he came from.

But at what price to Maddie?

"I'm not going to hurt her," he promised himself, standing on her front porch for a moment, watching the stars stud the skies over mountains that looked as if they were a silhouette cut from black paper and stuck against the sky. Why should he feel bad about saving everything she cared about?

"She's going to come out of this better than ever. She's going to be able to do what she most wants to do—save her world and everyone in it."

And if all of that was true, why did he feel as rotten as she had said his kiss was? Why did he wonder if, in the event she said yes, if she would walk toward him with all the enthusiasm of a prisoner being led to the gallows?

Lancaster hoisted himself off the car as he approached. He lifted an eyebrow in question.

"I asked her to marry me."

Lancaster looked stunned. "And?"

Ward said nothing.

"She said no?" Lancaster breathed with disbelief.

"Let's just say she didn't say yes. And you needn't look so pleased about it."

"My apologies, sir," Lancaster said insincerely.

"Spit it out," Ward said, then realized he had inadvertently used the same phrase she had used on him.

"She's strong and feisty, and honest and real. She's making you feel things you never felt before. It's all good."

"Unless I go home without a bride."

"I suspect your engagement to Princess Aida is over now, no matter what."

"You're so right," Ward said, and felt the relief sweep through him.

"But it's a good idea to bring home a bride. Insurance for Aida. If you called off the engagement, and her relationship with someone else came to light too soon, people would sense the truth. It would improve your popularity. But not hers."

"I don't want to hurt Aida. It has always been my intention to protect her. But I don't want Maddie to inadvertently end up hurt, either."

"Maddie's a good deal stronger than she looks, and she's good for you," Lancaster decided, looking at him shrewdly. "I hope she says yes."

"You've just an eye on the scones," Ward said, trying for a light note, but he was aware that was what he hoped for, too.

"I doubt if a princess would be baking scones for the likes of me," Lancaster said wistfully.

"I doubt if you could stop her," Ward disagreed.

"Yeah, she's that. Just a nice girl."

"Not all nice. She gave me the middle finger salute."

Lancaster laughed. "Ah, well, a little naughty mixed in with the nice could be a good thing. All sugar is a bit too sweet. You need a little spice."

"The middle finger," Ward mused. "I've never been on the receiving end of that before."

"You wanted to experience a bit of normal," Lancaster reminded him, wryly. "Not that the middle finger means what most people think it means."

"It doesn't?"

"No, in the old days the middle finger was the most important one on an archer's hand. If he was captured, it was cut off. And so when he won a battle, or eluded capture, he would extend his middle finger to the enemy to show *I will fight again*."

"I don't think she meant it that way," Ward said, drily. "Sod off, plain and simple."

"And yet to fight you again may be the way of her destiny."

"You're not leaning toward domestic bliss if she says yes?"

"What would the fun in that be?" Lancaster growled.

"Despite the scones, I don't see Maddie as traditional, the way our women are. But I like it, and I think it will be good for you. Once the initial shock is over, I don't think she's going to be cowed by the fact you're a prince."

Ward thought of the spark in Maddie's eyes when she unabashedly yelled at him, but, if she said yes, he was probably going to miss the sparks flying as part of a union with Maddie. Regrettably.

"It's not as if it's real, Lancaster."

"Aye, that's what you say."

"You sound doubtful."

"Just wondering, how do you keep it from getting real with a girl like that?"

"With great effort," Ward said. If she said yes, wouldn't that be the most important part of this exercise? Protecting her?

Lancaster was silent, he made no effort to get in the car. Ward realized he was faintly preoccupied.

"Something else on your mind?"

"Would you wait for me for a few minutes?" Lancaster said, glancing up the street.

"You'll leave me without your protection?" Ward asked drily, following Lancaster's gaze. "Is that Sophie's house?"

Lancaster looked torn. "I have to say something to her."

"Yes, you do," Ward agreed softly, and watched the big man lope away from him and knock softly on the door. It opened and he slipped inside, and it closed behind him.

Ward stood back and breathed in the crisp mountain air, the silence, the sense of being alone he had so rarely experienced. He was aware of freedom, the exhilaration of somehow being in control of his own fate, no matter what Maddie's answer was.

CHAPTER ELEVEN

MADDIE AWOKE IN the morning, aware of a shift in herself. It was the first time in a long time she had awoken without the feeling of dread in the bottom of her belly. Given the magnitude of the decision she had been asked to make, that seemed extraordinary.

She had thought she would have trouble sleeping, but instead, she had slept like a baby and awoken knowing her answer.

Oddly, it was not just about saving Kettle's business, Sophie's education and possibly, the town.

It was something more, a part of her she had been unaware she had.

There was in her a deep craving for adventure. A need for the unexpected. An embracing of this surprise life had offered her. She had not even touched her talisman, her pendant, seeking an answer, or reassurance, or a remembered voice to guide her. This had to be her answer, and hers alone.

Yesterday, she had been an ordinary girl, struggling with ordinary issues.

And today, that had all changed. Since the death of her father, Maddie had been so aware how life could change—for the worse—in a second, in the blink of an eye. That lesson had been reinforced, in the worst possible way, by Derek stepping out with a woman she counted amongst her best friends!

But this morning, she was aware it could change in the blink of an eye in other directions.

So she was going to say yes. Today, she was going to say yes to marrying a prince. She was going to marry a man who was a stranger. And one who had lied to her.

She was going to participate with him in the telling of an even larger lie. But there was a larger good here: both her town and the people she loved were going to benefit from this, as was a stranger named Aida. It was a wild adventure in saying yes instead of her customary no. So it was crazy to feel as calm as she did, as if she was marching toward that very thing he had mentioned last night: destiny.

She chose a simple summer dress, longer than the one she had worn yesterday, Indian cotton, pale yellow, buttoned down the front, belted at the waist, the skirt full and sensual as it swished around her legs.

She had no sooner tried to do something with her curls when she heard the soft tap at the door.

Taking a deep breath, she walked through her house to her door and answered it.

Ward stood there. He looked a different man. He was in a beautifully cut suit, a pristine white shirt, a navy blue silk tie knotted at his throat. He was freshly shaven, and he looked exactly what he was: wealthy, powerful, privileged. A prince.

It was as far from Maddie's own working-class background as you could get.

She contemplated, for the first time ever, the word *commoner*. Doubt attacked her, coming from all sides.

This was supremely dumb. It was hasty. It was fraught with emotional peril. Their arrangement was based on a lie. They were going to try and fool a whole nation.

In about five seconds, her mind chattered, rapid-fire, going through all one thousand reasons this was not a good idea in about five seconds.

But even as her mind chattered, there was a calmer place inside her. It regarded him deeply. It looked into his eyes and found something there she could both trust and hang on to in a world that had been so full of fear and disappointment.

"Yes," she said quietly.

Ward looked momentarily stunned, as though he had been bracing himself for a different answer. And then he smiled, and it was as if a light went on around them.

But then neither of them knew what to do! Did you shake hands on such an agreement? He took a tentative step toward her. Her eyes widened as his head dropped close to hers. Her heart went crazy.

But then he took both of her hands in his and bussed her lightly on the cheek, the way you might an elderly aunt you hadn't seen for a while! He let her hands go as quickly as he had taken them. Maddie felt oddly chagrined, even though she knew this was the safest way to treat their arrangement.

Though how were they going to make it seem as if they had experienced a wild, impetuous romance with kisses like that?

"I want you to know," he told her, "that though we will make a public appearance of husband and wife, you will always have your own sleeping quarters."

Don't blush, she ordered herself.

"I'll ensure your schedule is not too onerous, leaving you time to pursue your own interests and to explore the new world you will find yourself in on your own terms."

She nodded.

"I'll make sure you are generously remunerated for your time. Lancaster will work out the details with you."

"Thank you."

"And at every opportunity I will look for ways to promote Mountain Bend, and look for ways our business interests might benefit each other."

This was precisely why she had said yes. She took a deep breath.

"I'm sorry," he said. "A written contract might be complicated."

"That's fine." She stopped short of saying she trusted him. "What's next?"

"I have a private jet."

Of course he did.

"I've had Lancaster working on the logistics. We'll go to Las Vegas. No waiting period, and no difficulty marrying people who aren't citizens of the US. We can fill out an application online and be at the Clark County office to pick up a marriage license by this afternoon. An official will be lined up to conduct the proceedings."

She gulped. Had she been expecting things to unfold that quickly? *Not really.* On the other hand, it gave her less time to think, to lose her courage, to listen to that voice that was still insisting on rattling off the thousand and one reasons this was not a good idea.

"I need to talk to Kettle. And Sophie. I'll need to pack."

"Don't worry about packing too much," he said. "I can have someone come and pack for you."

She looked at him. It occurred to her he had probably not packed for himself *ever*. He had servants and staff who looked after all the mundane details of life for him.

"Why don't you see what you still need from here after I buy you a new wardrobe? We'll send someone with a list after you're settled."

She contemplated that. What did it mean? That her clothes weren't good enough? Obviously, they weren't good enough. She was wearing a cotton dress she had picked up on the sale rack.

And they'd send someone? From Havenhurst to Mountain Bend to pack her belongings for her? The easy extravagance of it took her aback. She could feel her feet getting colder by the second.

But suddenly, there was no time for second-guessing.

She quickly packed one overnight case, which Lancaster would not allow her to carry. He stowed it in the trunk of the car, and then they stopped at the Black Kettle.

"I'll go in alone," she told Ward.

"No, you won't."

"I don't know how much to tell them," she said, suddenly nervous.

"I think the fewer people who know the whole truth of it, the better."

She agreed. She set her shoulders and let Ward open the familiar door for her. She stepped in and looked around. Her home. This place had given her sanctuary from the world when she needed it most.

"You're late!" Sophie sang from the kitchen. "How unlike you. Guess who our ooh-la-la guys really are? It's all over town, and Lancaster confirmed it last night. He came to see me!"

Sophie came out the kitchen door and stopped, looking from Ward to Maddie, and then beyond them to where Lancaster was waiting outside.

"What's going on?" she asked.

"I—I—I'm going with them," Maddie said.

"I've asked Madeline to be my wife, and she's agreed," Ward said, taking her hand in his. Maddie was shaking. Was she going to be called Madeline now?

"What?" Sophie, naturally, was stunned. Her lip trembled. "Are you going to be a princess, Maddie?"

"I guess I am."

"That's fantastic," Sophie said, through tears. And then

Maddie found herself wrapped in a hug that was so tight that she could hardly breathe. That's why she was crying, wasn't it?

Kettle came out as Sophie broke away. Maddie told him her news.

Unlike Sophie, he was not prepared to see the romance of the situation. His face looked like thunder. "That's plain dumb," he told her. "You don't even know the man."

"Not that knowing the man served me that well," Maddie reminded him.

"Is that what this is about?" Kettle demanded. "Playing it safe? Taking yourself out of the game?"

Maddie hadn't thought about it like that, but was there some truth in what Kettle was saying? Love had let her down so badly, that she wasn't risking that again?

No, it was about being given an opportunity—to help her town, and those she cared about—and taking it.

Though she had a feeling if she said that to Kettle right now, he'd lock her in a closet and never let her out!

Kettle shook the spoon in his hand at Ward.

"I don't give a crap who you are—you hurt her, and I'm coming to get you. You hear?"

"Yes, sir, I hear. I won't hurt her. I promise."

Kettle limped over. He looked her up and down and then with tears in his eyes, he embraced her long and hard.

"Oh, Maddie," he said, his voice choked, "I thought you were going to be the sensible one."

"Are you and Sophie going to be able to manage? Without me?"

"We will," Kettle said firmly. "You'll step up to the plate, won't you, Sophie?"

The younger woman nodded solemnly. "Maddie, can I talk to you for a minute by yourself?"

"Of course," she said, and they went off to a table, leaving Kettle to grill Ward.

"Do you love him?" Sophie asked earnestly.

"Oh, Sophie, how could I know that? I just met him."

"But you're marrying him!"

"There are many good reasons to get married that don't necessarily involve love. Love's a funny thing, Sophie. I thought I loved Derek. And look how that ended."

"I love Lancaster," Sophie said firmly.

"Oh! You can't. Sophie, you're so young! You barely know the man!" Though given her own choice, that was a poor argument.

"Well, I do. When he came over last night, he told me something. He told me he thought I was a beautiful, smart girl, and that he didn't rebuff my affections—isn't that posh, rebuff my affections—because he didn't like me. He told me his wife and baby, a little boy, were killed in a fire. He said there's a stone where his heart used to be."

"That's very sad," Maddie said.

"It is *so* sad. But it just makes me love him more. Eventually, I'll come there, to Havenhurst."

"Of course you will!"

"And maybe he'll be ready," Sophie said, determination and wistfulness mixed.

"Maybe he will," Maddie agreed. "I'll call as soon as I'm settled. Maybe you can come in the fall, when things are slower here."

"I'm going to miss you so much," Sophie said, and then they were hugging and crying all over again.

When the hug broke, Sophie went and filled a bag with scones and a tub with cream. She handed them to Maddie, her eyes moist.

"Tell him they are a gift from me."

And then, their goodbyes finished, they were in the car

and heading down the road. Ward told her he thought it might be best if they didn't announce their intentions at all. Only Lancaster knew the truth of their arrangement, and he had arranged for the news to travel for them *after* they were married.

Before Maddie could really register what was happening, she was being ushered aboard a private jet. There was a crest by the tail: a dragon woven around a heart, and a crown above both of those things. The pilot and stewards and staff were all lined up at the bottom of the stairs, in navy blue blazers with that same crest embroidered above their breasts. As Ward ushered her by them, they each snapped off a crisp salute. She was pretty sure the shock of that would have made her trip and fall on her face if Ward did not have such a tight grip on her arm.

The inside of the jet looked more like a very fancy living room, than an airplane. Deep white leather sofas faced each other. Beyond the sofas, was a tall counter with a marble top. Shelves behind it showed a fully stocked bar, coffee, tea and kitchen items.

To one side of that, there was a desk with a deep leather chair on swivels facing it. And then there was a hallway that Lancaster disappeared down, still hugging his sack of scones with a look on his face that said he would protect that particular package with his life.

"Miss, my name is Glenrich, if you'll take a seat here," one of the uniformed attendants, a middle-aged woman with graying hair and a pleasant smile, told her, "I'll brief you on our takeoff procedures and see to all your needs on the flight." Already, an engine had thrummed to life.

Her needs? What could she need on such a short flight?

Ward took the seat beside her and showed her where the seat belts were tucked into the sofa.

Maddie only half listened to the safety talk, overwhelmed by what she was experiencing, the reality of it all around her. She wished Ward would take her hand, but he did not. In fact, he was brought a briefcase and immersed himself in papers!

The jet lifted off with such power, Maddie was sucked back into her seat. Moments later, she was being offered coffee and hot breakfast. She realized she was starving. The breakfast was superb, flaky croissants, homemade preserves, fluffy eggs. This was on an airplane!

Lancaster came back down the hall and settled in one of the chairs by the desk. He was now wearing a navy blue uniform, pressed shirt, with that same crest on the breast, tucked into crisply pleated trousers, which were tucked into black combat boots. He was clean-shaven and had an epaulette on both shoulders with three solid gold bars on each. What looked to be a beret was tucked under one shoulder bar, and there was a plain black dirk and holder on his belt. He said no to breakfast and tucked into the bag of scones, a notebook computer balanced on one knee.

He looked formidable, like a warrior, plain and simple, and had Maddie not been faintly intimidated by her surroundings she would have snapped a picture of him to send to Sophie.

"Miss Nelson," Lancaster said, appearing at her side with the small computer, "if you could fill this out, it will expedite matters substantially."

"Miss Nelson?" She didn't want Lancaster to call her Miss Nelson, but something in his face stopped her from inviting familiarity. She realized she had a whole new set of rules to learn.

The computer was open to the online application for the Clark County Marriage License Bureau.

"Your Highness, I've already filled yours out. Unfortunately, you both have to appear in person at the bureau to be issued a license."

Maddie slid Ward a glance. Was she supposed to address him as Your Highness? She was appalled at the thought and about how little she knew about the situation she was racing toward.

Was it unfortunate that they both had to appear because Ward did not normally have to do things for himself—not even fill out his own application—or unfortunate from a security standpoint?

"We should be there by noon," Lancaster went on. "You can marry immediately after being issued the license but I booked an Officiant of the State of Nevada for 4:00 p.m. I've arranged a suite at the Estate Hotel where the ceremony can be conducted. I thought it might be best if the two of you spent the night there."

Maddie could feel a deep blush darkening her cheeks. Good grief, the deception began. It was being made to look as if they consummated their marriage.

Ward nodded, then leaned forward and whispered something in Lancaster's ear.

"Yes, sir, my pleasure."

"Am I supposed to call you Your Highness?" she whispered when Lancaster had moved away and was out of earshot.

"I'll make sure you are fully briefed on proper protocol, but for now, there's no rush. I like it when you call me Ward."

And even though she was in a strange new world, those simple words made Maddie feel more at ease, a faint hope that maybe what she had agreed to wasn't complete insanity.

CHAPTER TWELVE

A REAL LIVE prince caused something of a stir, even in Vegas, where the marriage bureau saw everything and everyone from celebrities to Elvis look-alikes.

Despite an awestruck clerk, the license was issued quickly and efficiently. Then they were back in the stretch limo. Even in Vegas, where such vehicles were common, people were straining their necks trying to catch a glimpse of who might be inside.

The hotel, which looked like a Southern mansion, was an oasis of calm in the middle of that bustling, crazy city. They entered through a secluded garden and check-in was private and seamless, all handled by the Prince's unflappable staff.

The private plane should have prepared Maddie for the opulence of the hotel, but it did not. She explored the suite shamelessly. It was four thousand feet of pure luxury, and included two master suites, which given the *real* nature of their wedding night, was a relief to see. There was an indoor lap pool, a waterfall cascading down one wall and a huge fireplace, lit, even though the air-conditioning was on. There was a huge private deck.

Tables were covered with fresh flowers and pricey confections.

"I don't think I can get used to this," she confessed finally, meaning all of it—private planes and staff and VIP treatment and places like this. "Is your...er...home like this?"

"The palace is quite grand."

She gulped. His home was a palace. Her home for the next year was going to be a palace, too. It made her feel quite dizzy.

"But the palace is grand in a different way than this. This all seems quite new and glittery, the palace is more steeped in history and refinement. For instance, the table in the dining room is six hundred years old."

"I guess you wouldn't want to be spilling your red wine on that," she said.

He laughed. "I guess not. I think some of the table coverings are as old as the table."

She was beginning to feel like pressure was building up behind her eyes. On a good day, she wasn't even sure what fork to use!

Her drop into a new lifestyle was nearly immediate because the thing Ward had whispered to Lancaster about was apparently some serious pampering for her before her wedding. A whole team of professional pampering people arrived at the suite door and she was ushered into the smaller of the two master suites.

A massage table was set up, and before she knew it, modesty was cast aside, and she was under a sheet completely naked, being slathered in warm mud. The mud slathering was followed with her being wrapped in a thick white terry cloth robe and given a facial and pedicure and a manicure.

And then the door rocketed open, and a man swept in, pushing a clothes rack in front of him.

"Frederique is here," he called officiously. He abandoned the clothes rack and strode over to her. He took her chin in his hands and forced her head this way and that.

"Who are you?" she asked, pulling away from his hand.

"You don't know who I am?" he asked, aghast.

"I do not."

"Frederique, stylist to the stars." Then he smiled. "But also a long, long time ago, a young man who grew up on a little-known island called Havenhurst. Lancaster and I are childhood friends."

Somehow that was hard to imagine.

"I understand you are about to become *our* Princess." He said this with a certain frightening reverence, which, thankfully, was negated by his next words. "I see I have my work cut out for me."

"Thanks," she muttered.

"First, the hair. Did you cut it yourself?"

"Yes."

"Well, it's dreadful."

Maddie glared at him.

"So much to do, so little time." He lifted a lock of her hair and looked at it like a worm had attached itself to his fingers. "Maybe hair extensions," he muttered. "Except they take so long. A hair extension is a commitment," he told her sternly. "Are you prepared for that?"

"I think getting married is enough of a commitment for me for one day."

"Argh," he cried, throwing up his hands in frustration. But despite a rather major attitude, Frederique turned out to know what he was doing, and to be quite fun. He had "preshopped" for her and all the clothing on the rack he had wheeled in was for her to try on.

"How can you preshop for someone you know nothing about?"

"Five foot four and a half, approximately one hundred and eighteen pounds. What else would I need to know?"

Maddie gaped at him. How could he know that? Had Ward watched her that carefully? He had seen her in a bathing suit! She had seen him in one, too, but guess his weight? Accurately?

Frederique clapped his hands. "No time for lollygagging, love. Off you go. Start with underwear."

"I have my own!"

"I'm sure you do, and if it goes with that cheap little yellow dress, you will be needing new. I don't suppose you bought new for your wedding night?"

Maddie's mouth moved, but not a sound came out. See? This was where deception led you, straight into a more and more complicated web. What bride did not have new underwear for her wedding night?

"It's rather sudden," she said. "I guess I didn't think."

"Thank God for that. You would have ended up with precisely the wrong thing, I can tell by looking at you— sports bras and T-shirts. Gag me."

Happily, she thought.

"You do have potential, though. And I'd kill for the little bauble on your neck." Frederique reached out and touched her pendant, and then withdrew his hand. "Oh, how odd! It's warm."

Maddie touched it, too. The pendant was indeed warm, as if it was radiating.

"Here. Try this. And this and this." He tossed tiny pairs of lingerie at her, constructed primarily of silk thread spiderwebs. She retreated into the powder room and put on the lacy delicate items.

She stared at herself. She actually did have potential! The bra worked miracles with her modest bustline, and the scanty panties made her feel gloriously sexy. Had she ever allowed herself to feel that way before? Wasn't this bad timing? To be feeling sexy for a mock wedding night?

Still, she could not resist looking so feminine and pretty, and so she surrendered. Each outfit he passed her, she tried on. She saw the good underwear made the clothes look even more exquisite than they already were. She started to look forward to each outfit—a pretty cocktail dress, a colorful summer frock, a beautifully tailored pantsuit—and to twirling in front of Frederique's critical eye. He divided the bed into accept and reject piles and a large number of items were accumulating in both.

"That's way too many," she finally protested, surveying the growing stack of items to keep.

"Seriously, there is no such thing, but we are in a bit of a time crunch," he said, checking his watch.

Maddie was aware of feeling both exhilarated and exhausted, a thousand miles, literally and figuratively, from the girl she had been this morning.

"It's three, wedding is at four. A man could have a heart attack from this kind of pressure. Chop, chop, wedding dresses."

He opened the door and another rack awaited outside. On it were several selections of gorgeous dresses. He wheeled it in, took one off and put it aside. "I think it will be this one, but we'll try some others first."

"It's just a little private ceremony," she cried. Those dresses were something out of a dream, the kind of dress every girl longed for on her day of being a princess.

"Well, I understand there will be photos after, exclusive to three well-known media outlets. My reputation is at stake here."

Feeling trepidation, Maddie put on the first dress. Trying on wedding dresses was something every girl dreamed of. She had anticipated that day when Derek had proposed. Now, looking at herself in the floor-length white chiffon mermaid dress, she felt nothing, like an actress playing a role. Frederique walked around her, tapping his lip thoughtfully.

"No," he decided. "It doesn't work. Next."

He handed her another dress. It was a gorgeous champagne-colored ball dress. It didn't fit properly, and he had to pin the back of it. Again he circled her tapping his lip and squinting his eyes.

"No," he said. "Maybe for an evening wedding. Ach, as I thought, out of time. No more dillydallying!"

She could clearly see there was absolutely no point in addressing the fact she was not the one dillydallying!

He took the dress he'd put aside. "This one," he said.

She slipped into the washroom. The dress was white, the top fitted with laser-cut lace, dropping to a small belt, adorned with a silk bow. At the waist, the dress fanned out, an overlay of lace over an underlay of silk. The dress was tea length, and as Maddie looked at herself in the mirror, her eyes filmed over.

This was a dress for the girl she used to be: filled with hope, a believer in love. This was exactly the dress she might have once chosen for herself.

She suddenly felt sick that this was all fake, like a giant stage set. Had she really become so cynical she had accepted *this* instead of love.

Had Kettle been right? This, though it seemed crazy and bold, was really quite a *safe* choice? A fake marriage did not risk your heart, after all.

Unless you did something really dumb.

Like fall in love with him.

Meanwhile, it was a business arrangement. Help Kettle, help her town, maybe have an adventure in the process.

But all that made this perfect dress so bittersweet she wanted to weep. She took a deep breath and marched out of the bathroom. Frederique kissed his own fingertips and blew them at her. "Perfection. Now go take it off so it doesn't get rumpled." When she reemerged in the robe, he pulled out the chair at the dressing table. "Sit. Sit."

Maddie sat, sat.

And she watched the most amazing transformation happen. He started with her hair, each of the curls coaxed into good behavior until her hair was a soft wave around her face. And then he began with makeup: mascara and shadow, eyeliner, which she had never in her life used. Her eyes became astonishing: huge and green as a moss-covered forest floor. A sweep of blush here, and a sweep of blush there, and her cheekbones emerged, high and proud. He got out little pots of color, and with a look of furious concentration on his face, he painted her lips with a brush. Once, twice, three times.

She stared in disbelief as her lips became a shimmering, sensual invitation that said, without a shred of a doubt, *kiss me.*

As if in a dream, she stood and let the robe fall, while Frederique dropped the dress over her head, fussed with the bow and the hooks in the back. He knelt before her and inserted her feet into tiny white silk slippers.

And then he took a carved wooden box that she had not noticed on the bottom of the clothes rack.

"This," he said, bowing to her slightly, "is Prince Edward's wedding gift to you."

With shaking hands, she took the box from him and opened the lid. It was a tiara, encrusted in diamonds that shot blue flame into the room as the light caught in them.

"May I?" he asked softly. His own hands were shaking as he removed the tiara from the box and settled it on her curls.

She had expected it might feel heavy. Or silly. But it felt neither. It felt as if it fit her perfectly in every way.

Maddie regarded herself with astonishment. Dangerously, it suddenly did not feel as if she was playing a role at all. She felt as if, indeed, the magic wand had been waved.

She was Cinderella, turned into a princess for the night.

Frederique smiled. "May I be the first to congratulate you, Princess Madeline?" And then he bowed to her.

Without waiting for her answer, he went to the door and opened it.

Lancaster waited for her, in a full dress uniform of navy blue, resplendent with gold braiding and medals.

"I would be honored, Miss Nelson, if you would allow me to escort you."

She was so grateful for his solid strength, for his arm to slip her own through. She felt as if she was walking on air, as she and Lancaster made their way down the long hallway and into the main room, Frederique trailing them like a flower girl.

The room was empty, save for Ward and a woman in a gray business suit. They were chatting beside a desk, and Ward turned and looked at her.

Like Lancaster, he was in uniform, his jacket red with gold braiding, his pants navy and fitted. She looked into his face.

His handsome face was so familiar to her after such a short time. She remembered his shout of laughter as they hit the hot pools, and she remembered dancing with him at the concert, a man who had not been allowed to delight in small things.

But most of all, she remembered waking in his arms after she had fainted, the heat of his kiss still on her forehead, and looking into the deep blue of his eyes and seeing something there that a woman could hold on to.

That look was in his eyes now, as she walked—no, floated—toward him. He was looking at her, astounded by her transformation. He was looking at her as if he was a real groom and felt like the luckiest man in the world.

She shouldn't be feeling this way! And neither should he.

She drew up beside him. And then she turned slowly to face her future, and the man who would be her husband, Edward Alexander the Fourth, Prince of Havenhurst.

Briefly, she wondered if she would faint again, so huge was the welling of her heart. But then his fingers slipped under her wrists, and her hands were being cupped in his, and it felt as if he was coaxing every bit of strength in her to come forward.

And so Maddie heard her name and felt stronger and more certain than she had ever felt in her entire life.

"Madeline Elizabeth Nelson, please repeat after me."

She heard her voice, strong, confident, saying, "I, Madeline Elizabeth Nelson, take thee, Edward Alexander, to be my wedded husband, to have and to hold, from this day forward, for better or for worse, for richer or for poorer, in sickness and in health, to love and to cherish, till death do us part."

And then, his voice somber, made richer for the accent, he said those same words to her.

They were pronounced husband and wife, and they stood staring at each other in stunned silence.

"You may kiss the bride," the officiate said.

They stared at each other. What now? Lancaster cleared his throat when the silence dragged too long.

It was their first performance. Obviously both the official and Frederique believed this to be real. Both would probably talk about their experience.

Was that what Ward was thinking as he drew her closer? He stared at her as if asking her permission. She nodded.

He claimed her lips without hesitation, with mastery, with power, with passion.

Her first kiss from him—not counting the one on her forehead—did not disappoint. Everything faded save for the exquisite softness of his lips on hers. Everything faded save for the taste of him, which was as pure as forest dew. Everything faded save for the way she *felt*, which was on fire with life, which was as if every moment before this one had existed only to make way for this.

Connection.

Completion.

Ward broke the kiss and took a startled step back from Maddie, and she one back from him. She could tell he was as stunned by what he had just experienced as she was.

It was as if two souls intended for each other had met. The kiss had spoken in a language they, so new to each other, had not arrived at yet. *That* language was a language deeper than words, a language that shimmered along the skin, and charged the air they breathed with electrical current, and filled every space around them with the pure power and magic of possibility.

After it seemed as if they may have looked at each other with frightened wonder for way too long, she followed Ward's lead and turned to Lancaster and Frederique. The latter was wiping at tears.

Ward's hand found hers, and the *language* of his caressing her palm with his thumb was nearly as dizzying as that kiss.

Lancaster popped the cork out of a very expensive-looking bottle of champagne. Maddie felt as if she had already consumed the glass of champagne that was passed to her.

"A few members of the press have been invited," Ward said quietly, for her ears only. "They are waiting in the outer room. I thought it would be best if news of our marriage preceded our arrival in Havenhurst tomorrow. Would it be all right if they came in now?"

Maddie nodded, though she was stunned to be brought back down to earth with this reminder it was a pretense. This was what it was for: for show, for the cameras, and to save Aida, a girl Maddie did not know, a girl who was a *real* princess.

Not a fake created by Frederique.

CHAPTER THIRTEEN

WARD HAD FELT as if he was in a daze ever since he had seen Maddie walking toward him in that dress, looking gorgeous and outwardly composed. That pendant on her neck had been glowing as though it had taken on a life of its own. Though, when her eyes had met his, he'd known the outward composure was a show. She'd been nervous, and so had he.

The kiss had dissolved the nervousness and ushered in something far worse.

His desire for Maddie felt like a red-hot ember in his belly, and every time she glanced toward him, every time their hands brushed, it fanned the growing flame a little more.

When Lancaster bowed before them and offered his congratulations, Ward saw the slightly raised eyebrow, questioning the depth of the kiss.

Lancaster didn't speak it out loud, but he didn't have to.

Ward remembered their conversation all too clearly.

Just wondering, Lancaster had asked, *how do you keep it from getting real with a girl like that?*

Ward remembered how foolishly confident his reply had been.

With great effort, he had said with a certain nonchalance, as if yes, there would be effort, and no, not any temptations he could not overcome. He had known then, if she said yes, the most important part would be protecting her. He had promised Kettle she would not get hurt!

Well, she had just said *yes* and not any ordinary kind of yes, an *I do* kind of yes that felt bound up in tradition and honor and trust and faith.

But then along had come that mind-blowing life-altering kiss. Everything felt changed. His own power, which he had always been certain of, felt compromised.

Three carefully chosen members of the press waited in the outer room: coverage from one major magazine, one newspaper and one television network.

To invite the press was different for him. His whole life had been spent avoiding them, deliberately evading the spotlight.

But now he needed to use his position to get word back to his island kingdom before he arrived, so that everyone, including his father would accept this was a deal already done.

He thought of his father's great capacity for fury, and felt that need to protect Maddie grow in him.

Something cooled in her when they met the press, particularly as the television camera was set up. Lancaster read a prepared statement about how Prince Edward had been traveling in the US, incognito, with his vacation culminating in seeing his favorite band. In the small, pristine town of Mountain Bend, he had met an American girl who stole his heart, and after a whirlwind romance, they had married before his scheduled return to Havenhurst.

"How does it feel to be married to a prince?" Maddie was asked.

"Exactly like a fairy tale!" she responded, looking at Ward and smiling. He was sure only he could detect a certain tightness about her smile.

"Prince Edward, don't you have a fiancée?"

"Princess Aida Francesca has been informed of this turn of events," he said. Did Maddie flinch at the men-

tion of Aida's name? But why would she? He'd told her
the circumstances around their betrothal were less than
romantic.

"And how did she take it?"

"I know my answer will disappoint you," he said. "The
story would be better if there was a betrayed lover, with
weeping and wailing and gnashing of teeth, but nothing
could be further from the truth. Our arrangement was
contractual, and Princess Aida was surprised, but very
happy for me. She has always believed people should follow the dictates of their hearts."

Lancaster saw they wanted to press on the subject, and
so he indicated the interview was over. The magazine and
newspaper representatives took some photos, and then the
cameras were shut off and they were escorted out.

Lancaster told them quietly their wedding feast had
been laid in the dining room, and then took his leave also.

They were totally alone.

Maddie seemed to be avoiding his gaze, and she turned
and went to the dining room. She stood in the doorway
of the dining room for a moment, taking in the pheasant
under the glass cloche that kept it warm, the silver serv-
ing dishes, the exquisite place settings, the flowers in the
middle of the table.

"I'm not hungry," she said.

She sounded surprisingly like Belle in *Beauty and the
Beast*. The theatrical performance had come to Havenhurst last year and he had attended.

The story, he realized, shocked, was not dissimilar, a
girl who had exchanged her freedom for the promise of
her father's well-being.

He was surprised by how much he had hoped for her
company, but she brushed by him and went down the hall.
He followed on her heels.

"Maddie? What's happened?"

"I just miss Mountain Bend," she said.

He considered that. She had ridden in a private plane. She'd been pampered. She had been showered with gifts of clothing and jewelry. She'd had a feast laid out before her.

And she missed Mountain Bend.

Home. He tried to imagine what that felt like—that bond with the place where you felt sheltered and loved and understood. He had a bond with his island nation, to be sure, and a deep love for it. But a sense of home? Not so much, perhaps. She took a deep, brave breath.

"I think it would be best," she said, her voice strained, "if we didn't kiss again."

"I had the same thought," he said solemnly.

"You did?" Even though she had put it to words first, now she looked wounded!

How could he possibly have thought this wouldn't get complicated? Relationships were always complicated! And one that involved marriage? On paper, but not for real? With a woman who was extraordinarily beautiful and smart and exquisitely fragile, even though life had asked her to be strong?

"Unless you wanted to," he said hastily.

"I don't," she said firmly, "unless you want me to. For the press. Or whoever else you're fooling. About loving me."

He realized now would be a very bad time to remind her that this had never been about love. He'd told her that—any union he had would not be about love.

She thrust her chin up and he saw the hurt there. And then she slipped in her bedroom door, and snapped it firmly shut in his face. He heard the lock click, as if she felt she needed protection from him.

He stood there, utterly stunned. He had already broken his promise to both Kettle and himself. He'd already hurt her.

This was so different than any man's expectation for his wedding night that he might have laughed at the absurdity.

Not that, given the circumstances, he had expected a normal wedding night. But he'd been looking forward to her company, to getting to know her better. When he had seen her coming toward him in that dress, when he had drunk in the light in her eyes, he had actually had a moment when he thought it was all going to work out even better than he planned.

Truthfully, he had cast himself in the chivalrous role of using every bit of his strength to *just* get to know her better. And that did not include tasting those delectable lips again!

Now he saw it was Maddie who had done the right thing, the wise thing.

Still, when he thought he heard muffled sobs behind the door, he had to stop himself from kicking it in. He was the cause of those tears, after all. He'd been a married man less than two hours and already his bride was in tears.

He was sure that was probably a record of some sort.

Prince Edward was not sure he had ever felt as miserable in his entire life as he did, standing helplessly outside of Maddie's door, on the night of his wedding!

Maddie awoke the next morning, by herself in the luxurious bed, still in her wedding dress, which was now a crumpled ruin. She slid out of bed and went to her bathroom and looked at herself in the mirror. The makeup Frederique had so carefully and expertly applied had made raccoon circles under her eyes, which were a little puffy from crying. If she was not mistaken, there was a splotch or two of sooty black on the dress.

She should not feel for all the world as if she had a hangover. She had had one glass of champagne.

She touched her necklace. The gold still felt warm beneath her finger tips.

"Maddie Nelson," she heard her father's voice say sternly, "that is enough."

It was a reminder of what she came from: not royalty, but good, strong stock. She was a logger's daughter raised in a part of the country that prized toughness and resiliency.

Her father would have no patience with whining and even less for self-pity.

You made your bed, he would say, *now lie in it*.

So, she regretted that she had married the Prince? She had realized, a little too late, that his world was completely different from hers, and that the adjustments would be difficult? She was shattered that theirs was a business deal? Was shaken by what had been in that meeting of their lips?

"Too bad, Princess," she told herself, in her father's voice, and then giggled shakily, because she really was a princess.

She had made a deal, and she was not going to cry about it, or drown in regrets. She was not going to try and get out of the deal she had made.

That was not how she had been raised.

So she would perform whatever tasks were required of her to the best of her ability. She would not look longingly at her husband's lips, or give in to the longing to feel his hand in hers.

It was a job. She had accepted it, and she would do it.

She stepped into the shower and let the hot water wash away all of yesterday's angst. Today was a brand-new day.

Wrapped in a towel, she went and sorted through the clothes that Frederique had chosen for her. She put on the pale cream pantsuit, she blow-dried the curls out of her hair, she put on the lightest dusting of makeup.

She regarded herself in the mirror.

She didn't look like a princess, per se, not like she had in the wedding dress. But she did look calm and confident and ready for whatever was next.

Just before she opened the door, she made a decision and turned back into the room. She made the bed so expertly it looked as if no one had been there. Then she took the towels from the bathroom and the dress off the floor. She went across to the other master suite, hesitated, then knocked once briskly and entered.

Ward was in the bathroom. The door was open. He was standing before the mirror, with a razor in his hand, in a cloud of steam. He was dressed only in a towel. How she remembered those strong, sculpted lines from their day at the hot pools.

The longing rose up in her, but she quelled it quickly. "Good morning," he said, looking at her out the door, his eyes widened in surprise.

She dropped her wedding dress on the floor beside his bed, then surveyed the bed critically and rumpled up the sheets more than they were, then marched right by him and dumped her wet towels on the floor.

His eyes met hers in the mirror. She could not quite read his expression. Pity? Sympathy? Regret? Some combination of all three of those things?

"Good morning," she said crisply. "The maids might gossip if it didn't look as if we spent the night together. I thought we should make it look normal."

"Oh," he said. "Normal."

As if he had a clue what normal was! Ward had not

bought that razor in his hand. He'd never bought a razor. Or a tube of toothpaste. Or a roll of toilet paper. Everything in his whole life had been done for him. It gave him a kind of self-confidence, even in this totally awkward situation, that Maddie found extremely irritating.

Or was it kissing her until she had nearly lost her senses that made him feel as if he had the upper hand with her?

On her way out of the bathroom, she put her hand on the knot in that towel that was knotted at his waist and tugged. Hard. She felt the towel give under her hand, heard it whisper to the floor.

She didn't dare look back, but she had a feeling that look of aggravating self-confidence had been wiped entirely from his handsome face!

And that whatever he was feeling for her right now would not be even remotely related to pity!

From the bath and bedroom, she went to the dining room. The feast was untouched, but maybe that would make it look as if they couldn't keep their hands off each other?

A soft knock came on the door, and a key turned. Glenrich had arrived with breakfast things.

"May I congratulate you on your marriage, Your Highness?"

"Er...thank you."

"I'll pack your bags now, if that's all right?" she asked.

Another thing he didn't do. He didn't pack his own bags. Or do his own laundry. He'd probably never made himself a sandwich in his entire life. And now she wouldn't be doing those things either, and she was dismayed that she missed them already!

A third staff member came in, smiled, curtsied and handed her a newspaper.

"You look lovely, Your Highness."

Maddie stared at the picture on the front page of the paper. American Girl Marries Real Prince! the headline blared. But the picture was worth a thousand words.

She and Ward were gazing at each other with the look of two people madly in love, that wedding kiss they had shared still shimmering in the air around them. They looked like just the type of couple who would take advantage of Nevada's marriage regulations to impetuously get married.

Success.

If all went according to plan, only three hundred and sixty-four days to go.

She was going to need something to help her pass time. To get her mind off things. What had rescued her from every crisis she had ever faced? Helped her get through it? Provided reprieve from a reality that had become too hard to face?

Books!

She'd just pop down to the hotel store—startled, she looked up to see Lancaster blocked her way.

"I'm just going to go get a few books. For the flight," she told him.

He shook his head, ever so slightly, but it was still no. His eyes went over her shoulder, and she turned to see Ward behind them.

He was looking very princely, now that he had his clothes on! He was in a tailored shirt and jacket, a beautifully knotted tie at his throat. The shirt was brilliantly white. Did he ever dress casually?

"Good morning, Your Highness. I was just going to explain to your lovely bride why she can't pop by the bookshop. Perhaps you could take over?" Lancaster handed Ward the newspaper and Ward scanned it.

"Come have breakfast," Ward said, taking her elbow.

"I want to go get a book," she said dangerously, keeping her tone low. She extricated her elbow from his grip.

He held up the paper. "You can't."

"Can't?" she challenged him.

"I'm sorry. You were on the front page of the paper this morning, and possibly on the television news. You'll be recognized now. Everyone will want a picture of you. And there are others who would see you, unprotected, as a target."

Her mouth fell open and her arguments dried up. Her days of going out for a book were over? She was beginning to see why Ward did not buy his own toothpaste.

"If you'll give me a list of some of the books you'd like, or favorite authors, I'll make sure it's seen to," Ward said quietly.

Only three hundred and sixty-four more days.

Of imprisonment.

Her hand went to her necklace, as it always did when she felt uncomfortable, trapped, as if there was no way out.

One day, she could hear her father's voice say. *You feel like this after one day? Imagine what he feels like?*

Looking at his face, she realized this had been Ward's whole life. No wonder he had been so carefree in Mountain Bend. No wonder every moment had seemed to shine for him. She had never seen being able to buy toothpaste as a privilege before, but now that she couldn't do it, it did seem like one.

One she had taken for granted and he had never enjoyed.

Did she actually feel a tiny bit sorry for him? She did, and what was that going to do to her resolve to keep everything strictly business? Maddie's hand was still on the pure gold of her necklace.

What if, her father's voice said, gentle but with faint re-crimination, *it wasn't all about you? What if you, the girl who seems to have nothing, had something very precious to give him, the man who appears to have everything?*

It was true. Ward had exercised his power, so far, to make this a good experience for her. He had given her a spa treatment, and a whole wardrobe, and that gorgeous tiara.

On the other hand, what did she have, she asked herself. *What have I got to give a prince?*

You know.

And then she did.

CHAPTER FOURTEEN

As MADDIE HAD boarded the plane—her bags fully packed for her—Lancaster handed her a heavy sack. She peeked in.

A dozen or so books. She caught glimpses of some of her favorite authors' names.

"It's like having a magic wand," she told Lancaster. "I wave it and say, I'd like books please, and they appear. No saving money, no deciding which one you want the most, no going to the secondhand book store when cash is short."

"I'm glad you are pleased, Your Highness."

"I don't really like being called that," she said.

"Ah," he said, "you'll have to humor me."

"Watch it, or I'll wave my wand and turn you into a toad."

"Not your style," he decided with a smile. "Now if we gave Sophie a magic wand…"

They both laughed, and it felt good to laugh with him.

"Can you get me a deck of cards, too?" she asked.

"Poof," he said, as if making a deck of cards materialize would be the easiest thing in the world. If the request surprised him, it did not show in his face. If he had questions about the request, he did not ask them. If it was a problem to get her a deck of cards—as in it might delay the flight—he did not let on.

Maddie went to the same seat she had had yesterday and looked around. Already the awe factor was wearing off, already she felt less intimidated by the whole experience.

Ward boarded, acknowledged her with a faint salute and disappeared down a corridor toward the back of the plane. Did he intend to ignore her for the duration of the flight? Maybe for the duration of the marriage, except for public appearances? She frowned.

"What's back there?" she asked, when Lancaster returned.

"Prince Edward's office and private quarters."

"Hmmm."

He produced a deck of cards. "Solitaire?" he asked.

"That's a funny question to ask a newly married woman," she said. "No, I have other plans for these cards. Thank you for finding them. Which door is his office?"

Lancaster cocked his head at her. "Would you like me to ask when he can see you?"

"I'm not asking for permission to see my husband."

Lancaster regarded her thoughtfully for a moment, and then a faint smile played across his lips. "Yes, Your Highness," he said.

And she waited until he had taken his own seat some distance away from her to have a giggle at her own audacity. She could lose courage, though, and so as soon as the plane had leveled and the very subtle seat belt sign at the front of the cabin went off, she undid her seat belt, and holding her cards tight, she went down the same hallway that Ward had gone down.

She guessed at the door since Lancaster had not divulged that. Lancaster was watching her, but didn't try to stop her.

She had chosen the right door. It looked like the office of a successful executive anywhere: walnut paneling, a beautiful desk, a painting, no doubt priceless, hanging on the wall. It parted company with any executive office, because a door was slightly ajar, and through that was a bedroom, every bit as well-appointed as the bedrooms in the hotel they had just left.

Ward looked up, surprised, possibly a trifle wary.

"Hello."

She held up the cards. "Do you know what these are?"

"Playing cards?"

"Have you ever played cards?"

He frowned. "I don't believe I have."

"Well, it's going to be a long, boring flight for me, so I guess I'd better teach you."

He looked uncomfortable. As she had guessed, few people called the shots with him. "I was going to do some work, but—"

"What kind of work does a prince do?" she asked, taking the seat across from him at his desk, sliding the cards from their cardboard box and dividing the cards into two even piles, one in each hand.

"The island has many business concerns. I'm CEO of two crown corporations and a primary shareholder in several others. I also am the honorary head of several charities and the leader of our military."

She did a riffle shuffle—dovetailing the cards into a D-on-its-side shape—so that they cascaded down like a waterfall. "Military?"

"Mostly palace and personal security, but we also possess valuable resources that we protect, so we liaise and do exchange programs with other organizations, like the British SAS, Special Air Service."

She performed the same shuffle again.

"You're very good at that," he said, watching her hands on the cards.

"Yes, I am. That's what happens when you grow up a

logger's daughter in a town with long winters. You learn to play cards. Have you ever played poker?"

"I'm afraid not."

"Oh good," she said, "that improves my chances of winning."

"Isn't it a game of chance?"

"Some of it. Some of it is skill. I'll show you." She pulled her phone out of her pocket and went through her photos to a screen. "These are the hands and the values of each of the hands. So, clearly a royal flush takes all. Just like in your real life.

"So this is a simple form—I'm going to deal you five cards, and then you'll have three opportunities to discard and get new ones to build a winning hand. Here, we'll do a few dummy hands."

The Prince was intrigued, and caught on very quickly. As they played, she asked questions and found out as much as she could about Havenhurst: the population, the industry, the climate. She was learning and he was learning—and there was lots of laughter in between.

A staff member came in and put coffee and biscuits on the desk between them, then left. It made it hard to believe they were on an airplane!

"Does that happen all the time?"

"Coffee?" he asked.

"People sliding in and out, anticipating your every need."

"Oh." He looked surprised by the question. "I guess it does."

"Where will we be living?" she asked.

"I have a suite in the palace."

"Two bedrooms or one?"

"Four, actually."

"If anybody is going to believe this, Ward, there can't

be people sliding in and out all the time. They'd figure out pretty quickly that our marriage isn't a real one."

He looked perplexed. "I think I can trust my staff for discretion."

"Is that another way of saying who is going to change the toilet paper roll?"

He stared at her, and then he threw back his head and laughed. "That hadn't actually occurred to me. But I have a valet who briefs me in the morning."

"Well, he'll have to brief you somewhere else, because there isn't going to be any staff in our suite."

The laughter was still twinkling in his eyes. "Are you telling me how it's going to be?"

"I am. You can tell your staff it's a weird American thing. We don't like people hovering about, doing things for us that we are quite capable of doing for ourselves."

"The cook?" he said, hopefully.

"Your Highness, get used to scrambled eggs for dinner."

The hands went back and forth for a bit, and then she said, "Are you ready to play for real?"

"What does that mean?" he asked, a bit warily.

"Let's place a bet. Whoever wins ten hands is the winner."

"What's the bet?" he asked.

"I don't really have much of value. My necklace?"

"I couldn't take your necklace," he sputtered.

"You probably, literally, couldn't. You're not going to win."

He winced. "Still—"

"If you win it, I'll win it back from you next time we play."

It was in the air between them. Next time. This could be what their lives together were like, this casual banter, these easy conversations, this sense of building trust and friendship.

"No," he said, "if I win, I keep the cook."

"Okay."

"And what would you want from me?"

She smiled at him. "Diving lessons."

"Seriously?"

"Something wrong with that?"

Ward eyed his new wife warily. She had some surprises in store for him. The towel thing this morning had been a clear indicator of that.

"Choose something else," he told her firmly. "It's dangerous. For every dive you see that looks like the ones Lancaster and I did at the pools that day, there are a dozen or a hundred that didn't look like that. That have bruised and beat up the body. Lancaster has broken his nose and several ribs."

She looked properly frightened. He hoped that was the end of this conversation.

"Then why does he do it?" she asked. "Why do you?"

He hesitated. "I suppose there is a feeling of being alive that can't quite be replicated in other activities."

Wrong thing to say, apparently. She got that stubborn look about her that he was already beginning to recognize.

"That's *exactly* how I want to feel."

He saw he had walked himself into a trap. He had already said other activities did not quite replicate that feeling of falling through the air.

"Choose something else," he said firmly.

"Nope," she said, just as firmly. "Diving lessons. I'm sure you don't start on a ledge fifty feet above the pool."

He sighed. She could have asked for anything. The necklace she had offered him—the one that had deep sentimental value to her—also was probably worth several thousand dollars. She could have asked him for something in kind—a shopping trip, a bauble, an expensive perfume.

But she had not, and it told him a great deal about her. It also told him a great deal about her that she was not prepared to back down. People had been backing down from him for his entire life! If he said no, they acquiesced, immediately.

"Okay," he said. "Diving lessons. *But* starting very, very small."

She grinned at him, impish in her easy victory. Ward watched, fascinated, at Maddie's competence with those cards. He felt pressure to work—his in-box after his time off was overflowing—and yet he could not draw himself away from this fun time with her.

Even though she was exquisitely dressed today, and had done some awful thing to tame her hair, she was what he had seen least often in his life.

Real.

Genuine.

Normal.

And maybe most importantly, unintimidated by him. After their awful start last night, tears and slammed doors, he felt something like hope unfolding ever so softly within him.

They weren't going to be man and wife. He would not do that to her. He could not imagine any role stealing her lovely freshness, her ability to be genuine, more quickly than that one.

But maybe, just maybe they were going to be friends.

And most certainly, for a reason he did not understand, but felt grateful for nonetheless, she was going to give him little glimpses into normal, into a life he had missed and had given up hope of ever having. Though he hoped that meant his future wasn't full of toilet paper rolls, and that they were going to eat something beyond scrambled eggs.

The poker hands unfolding proved that they were both fiercely competitive. They shared laughs. He noticed how she was using this time to casually coax details about Havenhurst and his life from him.

He found out more about her growing up in Mountain Bend. They were, it would seem, getting to know each other. It was backward as could be to get to know each other *after* the wedding, but he was still enjoying it immensely.

He was not sure how, but the cards always seemed to land in her favor.

"Are you cheating?" he asked, throwing down his cards in disgust after she had taken six games in a row and there was no chance of him winning.

"Ah! The losers always ask that! When you're a little more certain around the cards, you'll be able to tell."

"You didn't answer the question," he pointed out drily.

"I can't wait to learn to dive!"

"Well, that should be a first. I've never heard of a girl diving on Havenhurst."

"Tell me about that, then. About the culture, about why a girl wouldn't dive on Havenhurst."

"It's probably because we don't have any swimming pools, and the rocky outcrops and high perches can be dangerous to dive from."

What had she let herself in for?

"Despite some changes because of the internet and television, we remain quite a traditional society," he said. "With quite traditional male and female roles. For instance, women tend to stay home with the children, while the men go out to work. The older people resist change."

"And you, are you traditional? Do you resist change?"

"I'm traditional in some ways." He didn't want her to dive, for one thing! "But in other ways, I feel it's my responsibility to shepherd Havenhurst into this century. The firstborn male son, at the moment, has more rights, say for inheriting land, than older siblings who are female. Even our monarchy is geared to a son taking the crown, not a daughter. I hope to change that in my lifetime."

"Are you that son?"

"Yes, I'll be King one day."

"It seems from another world," she said. "Like a fairy tale."

"It is another world," he agreed. "I'm not sure about the fairy-tale part."

"Is it at least charming?" she asked, leaning toward him, her chin cupped in her hands, so earnest.

"Charming. Aggravating."

"What do people do for fun?"

Fun. Not that that had been a big component in his life.

"We have a theater of sorts, and it's a big deal when we can entice the occasional live production to come in. The last one was *Beauty and the Beast.*"

"Does the theater have popcorn, like an American theater?"

"No."

"That's something I'll have to change," she said.

"Ah, your first royal proclamation."

He didn't tell her if they did get popcorn, he and she probably would not eat it, because the people had a certain expectation. And it was not to look up to the royal balcony to see a greasy-fingered prince and princess munching contentedly on popcorn.

"What else do people do for fun?"

"Well, we have hot pools literally everywhere, and so

that's a big part of island life—taking a picnic to one of the pools. But mostly entertainment is the party, the cei- lidh, gatherings of people in kitchens and pubs, where they play homemade instruments, and games. Singing and dancing and lots of imbibing."

She looked at him, hearing something he hadn't said.

"You don't do that, do you?"

"No."

"Not ever?"

"No."

"Are you a lonely man, Prince Edward?" she asked.

He stared at her. Just like that, she had cut through to the emptiness in his heart. Just like that, she had uncov- ered a longing in him that could not be met.

"You ache to belong, don't you?"

"It's not what I was born to," he said, deliberately hard- ening his voice.

This would be the problem with her: she would ask questions of him that he did not want to answer, she would stir longings in him that were best left sinking way below the surface.

Even this: playing poker, having a normal conversa- tion, he could not give in to it. It would only lead to more wanting.

Wanting more from her than he could ever ask her to give him.

Now was the time to set limits, to remind her how it was going to be: a business arrangement between them.

He could not afford to indulge in more than that. To let his weakness out, his secret hopes, his longing.

To have a lass look at him, just the way Maddie was looking at him now.

"This has been great fun," he said, his voice firm,

"but having lost my shirt at poker, I must now get back to work. Duty calls."

She looked slighted.

She looked hurt.

It was what he had promised Kettle he would not do. But here was the question: hurt her a little now, or a lot later?

Because that's all that could come of it if he let down his guard around her, let her behind the closed doors of his world.

Yes, there would be riches. The baubles and the privileges, the jets and the yachts.

But Maddie had already shown she had little taste for those things.

And if he drew her into his world—if what they had pretended ever became real between them—every other door would be closed to her.

She would stand on the outside, as he did, listening to the laughter and the music of the ceilidh without ever being invited in to experience its warmth.

There was no sense her not knowing the absolute truth of his life: duty *always* called.

She only looked hurt for a moment. And then she touched that gold nugget necklace that never left her neck, smiled, stuck out her tongue at him and flounced from the room.

Stuck out her tongue at him.

Did she not know he was a prince?

Of course she knew. And it was so refreshing that she didn't care. But he could not allow himself the weakness of dipping into that pool of freshness that her guileless eyes offered. Really, this all would have been so much easier if Sea had not let him down.

He sighed heavily, turned to his work. As if to affirm

his decision to distance himself from Maddie, there was a scathing email from his father, who had just heard the news of his marriage and berated him soundly for his betrayal of his duty.

It was this world that Ward needed to protect Maddie from. He had promised.

Ward put his head in his hands? Who would ever invite a woman they actually liked to share this kind of life? If Aida married quickly, he would find a way to release Maddie before a year was up.

Because he felt more strongly for her with each passing moment, with each encounter. His heart sank when he thought what he might feel like after a year. He had to keep his distance or he was never going to be able to let her go.

And even having made that vow, when the jet began its descent toward Havenhurst, he found himself going to be with Maddie. Somehow, he did not want to miss her first reaction to his island home.

"It's beautiful," Maddie breathed as Ward materialized at her side and buckled himself in, in preparation for landing.

As she watched out the window, the jet circled her new home.

"I've asked them to fly low and circle, so that you can see it from this perspective," Ward told her.

From the air, the island of Havenhurst was absolutely gorgeous: lusciously green from its neat fields, to forests, to carpeted mountains. From the air, she could see it was dotted with turquoise pools and cascading waterfalls.

"The carpets of pale purple around the pools?" Ward pointed out. "Those are wild lupines."

They flew over three villages, which he named, but when she tried to repeat the names after him, they both ended up laughing. She could see thatch on the stone cottage roofs and winding cobblestoned streets.

"This is the main city, Breckenworth," Ward said. Maddie pressed her nose against the window and looked down at a place out of a fairy tale. A thick stone wall surrounded a town with soaring church spires and Gothic-style buildings, interspersed with neat pastel painted cottages and row houses and shops. The greenish slate tile roofs shone from a recent rain. Narrow streets wove, with seeming randomness, through the city.

"It's absolutely charming," Maddie said.

And then, the plane swooped upward, and she drew her eyes away from the town. On what appeared to be a rock with a sheer cliff face, overlooking the town was a magnificent Gothic-style castle. The closest she'd ever been to a castle was the Sleeping Beauty Castle at Disneyland. This one looked remarkably similar with its soaring towers and spires, its intricate maze of walls and interconnecting buildings.

"If you look closely," Ward said, "you can see a staircase carved into the stone cliff from the castle to the town below."

"Oh my gosh, I hope that's not how the groceries are brought in!"

He laughed as they flew up and over the castle, revealing stables and car parks, fields and forests, stretched out on a plateau behind it.

She could also see the airfield they were landing on. She gasped. It was surrounded by people!

"How many people did you say are on the island?" she asked.

"A million."

"Are they all here?"

"Possibly," he said, wryly. "They'll be wanting to catch a glimpse of their new Princess."

"Word traveled fast."

"For a place with little internet, you'd be amazed."

She looked down at her now-travel-rumpled suit. "I'm changing," she said, and tried to get up.

"You'll have to wait until we've landed." Ward's hand slipped into hers. She took a deep breath and felt the reassuring pressure of it.

She wasn't sure if she should feel this way, because really, what had he done to earn her trust? In fact, he had dismissed her just a short time ago!

But then she thought of all the effort he had made to make her wedding day perfect, despite the pretense, and she thought of how gamely he had played poker, and she let herself relax a tiny bit. He was a strong man; it was okay to rely on that when meeting a million people!

Maddie was shown to where her things were: an opulent bedroom across the hall from Ward's office. Her suitcases were there, and suddenly she was grateful for the quiet assistant, Glenrich, who took her choice of dress and quickly steamed the wrinkles out of it. It was a very simple burgundy dress with a matching short jacket. Even though the low heels were brand-new, Glenrich quickly swiped them with a cloth that brought out a deep shine in them.

Maddie went and stood by Ward at the door of the plane. He too had changed. And shaved. He was wearing a navy blue suit with a white shirt, that made him look powerful and calm and confident and as though he owned the earth.

But of course, he did own this earth!

"Ready?" he asked.

Lancaster was there, behind her, and spoke in her ear,

"The Prince will descend the staircase first. He'll stop at the bottom and take your hand. He will hold hands with you, and you'll go left to the fence that holds people back. Shake a few hands, one light pump and withdraw, or your hand will ache for a week. Exchange a word or two, keep moving. If you accept flowers, hand them off to Glenrich after you've admired them. Watch the Prince. When he makes his way to the car, follow."

"Is everything this choreographed?"

"It's not all eating bonbons and attending balls," Lancaster said mildly. "Glenrich will be putting together a protocol book for you, which should prevent any major gaffes. It remains to be seen if the people will take to you more or less because you're an American."

The door of the plane opened, and Ward stepped out. A roar of approval shook the ground as he raised his hand.

Maddie realized this was the last time he would feel like Ward to her. He was their Prince, and everything about him, from his stance, to his raised hand, made him Edward Alexander the Fourth, the future King of this small island.

As they went down the stairs, a chant began to build.

She was stunned to hear what it was.

"Princess Madeline! Princess Madeline!"

It was as if one huge voice called her name. It made her want to shrink behind Ward, to turn and run back up the steps to the plane. But the way was blocked with Lancaster and staff coming behind her.

Ward stepped to the right, exposing her for the first time. He took her hand.

A great, approving cheer went up from the crowd, his abandonment of Aida apparently already forgiven in favor of a love story.

The chant changed. "Kiss! Kiss! Kiss!"

He turned to her. Their eyes met. They had promised each other no more of this, but it was evident the crowd was hungry for romance. His eyes asked the question.

She nodded, her heart beating harder than it had when she had seen how large the crowds were.

He dropped his head over hers, and the crowd went wild.

The kiss was not as lingering as the wedding kiss had been, but still Maddie was so aware of how she loved the taste of him, how it filled her with a sense of a rightness in the world. And that was what she carried with her as they went forward to the crowds that pressed against a steel, waist-high fence.

She shook hands, she accepted flowers, which she buried her nose in, before handing them to Glenrich. She could not stop smiling as the love and approval washed over her. They welcomed her. They congratulated her. They wished her the best. They said how they loved their Prince and wanted a happy life for him.

She didn't really need any words, beyond thank you.

The experience was so lovely it was actually very difficult to remember this was not real: that she was not his bride in the sense any of them thought she was.

Maddie and Ward, finally, made their way to a waiting car, a beautifully restored Rolls-Royce. A uniformed driver held the door for her, saluted the Prince. They turned, as a couple, and waved one last time.

One tiny old lady was holding a baby over the fence, and Ward dropped Maddie's hand, ran over, scooped the baby from her and kissed it on the cheek. The crowd roared their approval as Ward handed the baby back.

Maddie noticed Lancaster, watchful, but relaxed as Ward came back toward them.

"I am a little overwhelmed," she confided to him, in

a quiet aside. "I don't know what to do with this kind of adoration."

"You do what he does."

"Which is?"

"You earn it, every single day."

That single statement gave her a very different perspective of the man who was walking back toward her.

They drove away from the airport, leaving the crowds behind them. Then the car was on a road, lined with mature trees that formed a canopy of green over it. At the end of that tree-lined roadway was a courtyard, a wide staircase, and the main entrance to the castle.

A spectacular fountain shot geysers of water into the air in the center of the courtyard. The car floated to a stop at the bottom of the stairs. Staff, dressed mostly in white uniforms, lined both sides of the steps, and at the top stood a man and a woman.

"Your father and mother?" Maddie asked with a gulp.

"King Edward the Third and Queen Penelope."

"I guess I don't refer to them as Mom and Dad?"

The Prince hid a smile.

Lancaster was at her ear. "When you reach the top of the stairs, drop the Prince's hand, curtsy and address them—first His Majesty the King, and then Her Majesty the Queen."

"I don't know how to curtsy," she whispered.

"Maybe poker-playing time could have been better used, Your Highness," Lancaster suggested drily.

"I'm afraid I wouldn't trade that time for anything—not even making a perfect first impression on my new in-laws."

Lancaster eyed her sternly, but she could see laughter behind his expression. "Do not offer your hand. If either of them offers theirs, you may take it."

Ward's hand tightened on hers as they walked up the steps. Unlike the warmth that had radiated from the people who had greeted the plane, there was a definite chill in the air here.

At the wide platform at the top of the steps, Maddie offered an awkward curtsy, and the acknowledgment of their titles. Neither offered their hand. Ward's mother was extraordinarily beautiful, but her eyes were remote, and her mouth had the downturn of perpetual bad humor about it. His father radiated a kind of power that was not like the kind of power Ward radiated, but his eyes seemed cold as they assessed her, and it was everything she could do to prevent herself from shivering.

Though of course they would be irritated with Edward going against their plans for him and choosing his own bride in America, Maddie found their greeting to him to be stunningly chilly.

And then the King and Queen turned their backs on them and swept away, the doors of the castle opened by two servants in matching livery, and then closed behind them.

"I take it we haven't been invited for tea?" Maddie said in a low voice. She was scanning Ward's face.

There was a look on it as remote as the look on his mother's had been, as if he had not been hurt by the remoteness of the interchange and by the total lack of welcome for his new bride.

"Come," he said, his tone crisp and level, "I'll show you our suite."

"Are they always like that?" Maddie asked, as they descended the stairs.

"Always like that? No. Usually, they're worse."

She stared at his face. It was cast in cool lines. She had hoped he was kidding, but she could see he was not.

Suddenly, unexpectedly, she ached for this man who was her husband. She had already seen that he lived a life constantly surrounded by people, who clearly worshipped the ground he walked on. And yet none of them were his friends, though obviously he was as close to Lancaster as anyone. Still, his station in life separated him from others. He'd grown up with that, accepted it, and as far as Maddie could see, had no expectation of anything else.

But somehow she had assumed that he had family who loved and supported him, who formed his clan, his safe place, his soft place to fall.

She thought of the remoteness of the couple she had just met, and she could clearly see nothing was further from the truth.

She touched the beautiful warm gold stone on her neck.

Another woman might have wondered if she had impulsively allowed herself to be dropped into a nest of rattlesnakes.

But that was not how Maddie felt. Not at all. Audacious as it was, Maddie thought perhaps she wasn't here to save her town. Or to have an adventure.

Perhaps she was here on Havenhurst to rescue a prince.

CHAPTER FIFTEEN

WARD LED HER around the side of the castle and through a lush garden. It was filled with early roses, and well-kept beds of rich, dark loam. There was a stone bench and an exquisite fountain that bubbled happily. But what was the point of a happy fountain and gloriously blooming roses—what was the point of all this beauty—if everyone was miserable?

His suite was past the gardens, and under an arch that dripped with purple-flower-laden wisteria. She craned her neck to see the plant went up over the arch and climbed the castle walls. It seemed it must be nearly as old as the castle.

He went through a door and held it for her.

"Welcome," Ward said, watching her face.

They had entered a vestibule with carved wooden wainscoting that gleamed from polishing. Beyond that was the living room, and she stepped into it as if she was a guest looking at a roped-off room in a museum.

It was gorgeous, of course, with high ceilings, a glorious chandelier, an enormous fireplace and tufted silk sofas facing each other over a low glass table that sported a huge vase of fresh flowers. All of this sat on a large square Turkish rug that was probably priceless. Everything in the entire room looked very elegant and very old.

"But where do you curl up with a book and a cup of tea?" she asked.

"I want you to do whatever you need to do to feel at home."

She wondered if there might be a garden shed somewhere she could make into a little reading spot. She could not ever imagine feeling at home in this expansive room.

Over the fireplace hung a portrait of an extremely stern-looking ancestor. He was positively glaring at her from his gilded frame.

"Good grief," she said. "Is this a relative?"

"Great-grandfather—King Edward the First."

"Is everyone in your entire family miserable?"

He laughed with surprised enjoyment. "Is it that obvious we aren't exactly—" he paused, obviously searching for a reference, and then brightened as he found it "—the Brady Bunch?"

"No one's the Brady Bunch," Maddie said. "But a family is supposed to be—how should I put this?—your safe place, in all the world. The place where it's okay to be yourself, and to make mistakes, and people get mad at each other from time to time, but underneath all that it flows like a river that will never stop."

"It?" he said quietly.

"Love," she whispered, and somehow she was afraid to even say that word in such close proximity to him.

She barely knew him. They barely knew each other. But they were going to. And love had a way of finding its path, of always breaking rules and refusing to be defined, because when she looked at him, her heart felt something.

Something sweet and pure and lovely that wanted desperately to rescue him from his loneliness. If she followed these impulses, they were going to lead her to a place where the potential for hurt was enormous.

But also to a world that felt brighter and more hopeful than it had before. A world that made her over into something different than she was now: someone more complete, more connected. More *everything.*

Ward's laugh was so world-weary it made her heart ache.

"Love?" he said cynically. "Love would be seen as a weakness in this family."

So it was true. Maybe she was here to rescue him. But at what risk to herself? The thing about love was it was so brave. So darned brave. It didn't care if you'd been wounded before. It threw itself down at the feet of possible catastrophe and it said *Stomp on me, tear me up. I don't care. It's worth it to feel this way.*

Love beckoned; it whispered *I am stronger than that imagined catastrophe. I am stronger than anything. Give me a chance and I will win.*

She turned hastily away from him. One day into her marriage of convenience and she was already in the thrall of something that felt much larger than herself.

Maddie shamelessly explored every inch of the suite. It wasn't huge, though it was obviously way more than two people needed. Besides the living room there was a formal dining room with a table that could sit sixteen, a homey kitchen with a table in it. She took a quick look in four luxurious bedrooms, but didn't explore too deeply because one of them must be his, even though they all looked equally unlived-in.

After she had finished looking around, she found Ward in a book-lined study. It was possibly her favorite room!

"Well?" Ward asked. "What do you think? Can you feel at home here?"

"Can I really do what I want?"

"Of course."

"I'd like to get rid of the grim paintings of old men glaring down. The fixture with the dragon in the entry has to go. It could give nightmares. And the curtains are awful. So dark and heavy. They cut the light dreadfully."

"And keep out drafts in the colder weather," he said. "You'd be surprised how hard it is to keep a castle warm October to March."

"Hmmm. I bet there's a lot of babies born here May to September," she said and then laughed at the surprise on his face. Was he blushing, ever so faintly? Devilishly, she liked that!

"It's obvious there's staff, but I'll have to kick them out to feel at home."

"Of course," he said, but she heard a trace of doubtfulness in his voice. "Whatever you need to do to feel comfortable."

Her eyes slid to his lips. And she could have sworn he was blushing again, but he turned away from her quickly.

"Which bedroom should I take?"

"Let me show you." He got up from his desk and led her down the hall.

"See if this room suits," he said, opening the door of one of the bedrooms she had only glanced at earlier.

The room was like something out of a movie, particularly the huge four-poster bed in the middle of it. It looked as if a family of eight could sleep comfortably. Still, there was a faint heaviness to the room. She would get rid of the dusty tapestry that lay heavily across the bed, and she'd have to put the delicate porcelain figurines away. She'd live in fear of breaking one if she didn't.

She hated the painting on the wall above the bed, a dour woman whose eyes seemed to be following her with pure malice. She shivered. "Another relative?"

"That would be a great-great-great-aunt—Mary. She's said to have been rather nasty. Ran her husband through with a sword while he slept."

"She is leaving right now!" Maddie went right over to the bed, jumped up on it and lifted the framed canvas above it off the wall.

It was heavier than she had thought it would be, and once it was in her hands she found it hard to get her footing on the soft bed. ,

"Drop it," Ward said, and when he saw she wasn't going to listen, he hopped on the foot of the bed and lurched toward her. The mattress bounced with his added weight and bounced more as he made his way across the bed to her.

"Oh," she said, unsteadily, "oh, dear."

She released the painting, and he went to catch it, but then realized he had to catch it or her. He chose her, but it was too late.

Her legs had collapsed under her. Her momentum pulled them both down in a hopeless tangle of limbs, him on top of her. He managed to deflect the painting from hitting them, but she heard it hit the floor with a distinctive crunch.

Maddie stared up at him and felt his weight on her, most of it being held off, but still enough that she could feel the uncompromising lines of him, be nearly overwhelmed by his gorgeous scent.

She freed an arm and touched his face. He had shaved before getting off the plane and his skin was smooth, as sensuous to touch as silk. She traced the line of his lips, the lips that had kissed her so recently, and felt a surrender sigh within her. She loved how the blue sapphire blue of his eyes deepened to the navy blue of deep seawater as he looked down at her.

"Maddie?"

"Yes?" she whispered.

"I don't think this is a good idea."

"It wasn't really an idea. More like an occurrence."

His mouth tilted up on one side. He really had a sinfully sexy smile. The expression on his face was one of amazed discovery. *Of her.* With exquisite softness, he traced the line of her mouth.

They heard a door open.

He leaped off her. "That will be the luggage. Should I send it in?"

"Tell them to leave it at the door. We don't want them in here, Ward. Or they'll know."

But know what? It certainly didn't feel like a sham at the moment! He gave her one more faintly tortured look and disappeared out of the room.

Maddie's first weeks at the palace passed in a blur. She wasn't sure if Ward had planned it like this to minimize "occurrences," or if he'd done it to keep her from feeling lonely, or if this was simply the pace of his life, but it seemed every moment of every day was highly scheduled.

She barely saw her husband, let alone had an opportunity to "rescue" him from what she had perceived as his loneliness. Now it was clear he was far too busy to experience the normal pangs of human loneliness. She was not sure she had ever seen a man who started so early in the morning and worked so late. Was he avoiding her? Or was he always like this?

But her own life was also a whirlwind. Mornings were devoted to the wedding gifts and cards that had begun to pour in from around the world. Edward's sister, Princess Abigail, sometimes dropped by to help, her precocious daughter, Anne, with her. Though Abigail was reserved, Maddie soon delighted in the visits because of Anne.

Glenrich became her lifesaver. Though much of what was sent was presorted, every gift received had to be acknowledged with a signed card. Many of the gifts were extremely valuable, and Maddie had to decide what to do with them. Some were adorable, like the one from a six-year-old girl in California who sent her a plastic tea set for hosting her princess parties! She passed that along to Anne, who treasured the plastic set above her many, many rare and expensive toys.

During those mornings, Glenrich coached her, gently and firmly. Protocol. What to wear for what occasion. How to address whom, in public and in private. When did you shake hands, and when didn't you? The proper way to hold a teacup. And a knife and fork. There was even an accepted way for her to sit, her legs never crossed, but pressed together and leaning to one side, her hands clasped neatly together in her lap.

Glenrich also taught her a few words of the ancient language of Havenhurst, particularly old greetings, and words of thanks and sympathy. She taught her the colorful history of the island and helped her sort through the mind-boggling number of invitations she received.

Maddie was so grateful to Frederique that she had a suitable outfit for every occasion, for every day held occasions. She was the Prince's wife, and people wanted to meet her. Glenrich, thankfully, slipped into the role of her secretary. Having her own staff member increased the sense of this all being a dream. In what world did Maddie Nelson from Mountain Bend have a secretary? In this world, where she desperately needed one.

Maddie's favorite events quickly became the ones she attended with Ward, since she seldom actually saw her husband and got to spend time with him. It was with growing amazement she watched his skill with people. He treated everyone—from the flour-covered baker walking down the street, to high-ranking officials—with equal respect. He made time to listen. He engaged people at a deep, deep level. The admiration of the palace guard soldiers was obvious, as was the affection of every member of the palace staff.

He was also treated with extraordinary respect and not entirely because of his station. She could tell his skill at business was extraordinary and his investment in the future of his island was all consuming.

In private he was unfailingly decent and respectful to her, winning her trust and her admiration day by day, and yet she found she was beginning to like the public occasions, because his affection came out. Maddie loved the feel of his hand resting on the small of her back, the way he teased her, the way he cocked his head to listen to her, the pride in his voice when he introduced her to someone. He made her feel special, but of course, he did that to everyone.

It was what she had signed up for, and yet she felt disappointed that the small gestures were dropped at their front door. They barely shared the suite.

The truth was her husband was winning her heart the same way he had won the hearts—the absolute devotion—of his people. But she wanted more.

She was the one who wanted a change in the rules!

And when she received a handwritten invitation, addressed to her personally, to Princess Aida's wedding, she hoped she had found a way to do that.

CHAPTER SIXTEEN

PRINCESS AIDA'S WEDDING was small, perfect and beautiful. She and her groom had invited only a few select guests. Despite that, for privacy, they had secured an entire lodge on the Island of Wynfield. Everything had been set up at a grotto around a pool, and once the ceremony and meal were finished, the tables were put away and music and dancing ensued.

Aida and her husband, Drew, were so in love, and so open in that love, that Maddie was envious.

Ward was particularly handsome tonight, in a black tuxedo, white silk shirt and bow tie. He knew all the people there and was so skilled at including Maddie in the conversations that she soon felt that she had known them all her life, too.

They had not danced together since the concert.

Now, when they did, Maddie was so aware how much her feelings for him had changed. But just like that night, she felt sexy and beautiful, and she loved it that she could tell by the look on his face that he found her sexy and beautiful, too.

They laughed and danced and talked until the wee hours of the morning. It was the most time they had ever had together.

As they were preparing to leave, Lancaster appeared and whispered something to Ward.

He turned to her. "I'm afraid there's been a small

mechanical problem with the plane. It will be fixed by morning."

It occurred to her they would be staying here! And that they couldn't very well ask for separate rooms.

Maddie was thrilled. She couldn't wait to have her gorgeous husband to herself. She could not have planned for the evening to end this well.

They entered the room, and both of them gaped. It was like a honeymoon suite: a beautiful four-poster bed at its center, draped in white gauzy fabric. There were even rose petals scattered on the cover.

"I'll sleep on the floor," Ward volunteered.

But Maddie was tired of Ward being the gentleman. Tired of the distance between them. She craved a deepening of their relationship, in every way. She took his hand and pulled him to the bed, sat down and patted the place beside her.

He hesitated, and then sat.

She spoke no words. She placed her hand on the back of his neck and drew his lips to hers.

She tasted him, well aware this was their first kiss that was not public. This was their first kiss that was not for display. It felt as if she had waited her whole life for this kiss. She felt like a flower that had waited for rain, as if her petals, dry and thirsty, were opening up in celebration of the force that gave life.

He groaned with surrender, wrapped his hands in her hair and pulled her in tighter to him. The kiss became savage with need. He pushed her gently onto the bed, and lay down over her, covering her body with his own. Her every cell felt as if it was screaming with need of him. She let her hands roam the hard surfaces of his body. She reached for the buttons on his shirt.

He rolled away from her, sat up on the edge of the bed,

and then found his feet. He ran his hand through the dark crispness of his hair. His chest was heaving. His eyes were dark with wanting.

But he looked tormented.

"I can't," he said huskily. And then he turned sharply on his heel and left the room, closing the door with a quiet snap behind him.

What? What had he seen, naked in her face, that he knew he could not—or would not—return? It was a warning, and she wished she could heed it. His family, after all, saw love as a weakness. She had thought she could knock down his barriers, but now she was not so sure that her growing feelings for him could break down the barriers he had put around his heart.

Or maybe it wasn't him, at all. Maybe it was her. It seemed every insecurity she had ever had rose to the surface. She wasn't good enough for him, just as she had not been good enough for Derek. She let the tears fall.

Edward made his way through the dark streets of Wynfield to the airport. Lancaster, with his instinct for these things, had somehow materialized and dogged his heels down the dark streets, but did not try to engage him in any conversation.

Edward decided he would stay on the plane tonight. He could not believe what had just happened. He was a man who had been raised knowing the virtues of control. He had known, practically since he was a toddler, how to control himself. As he had grown older, he had learned how to control the world around him.

And yet, just now, with Maddie's sweet curves nestled underneath him, with her eyes wide on his, with her lips moist and full, he had nearly lost control completely.

Oh, not the *me Tarzan, you Jane* kind of control,

though, yes, her lips beckoned and he had given in to the temptation to taste them. And taste them. And taste them. It was like drinking a wine you could never get enough of.

But it was a different loss of control that he feared even more than the desire that burned like a hot coal in his belly anytime he was within touching distance of her.

He had seen something in her eyes. Something to reach for. Something to believe in. Something to trust. Something to hope for.

He had seen what she was offering him: a lifeline.

The shocking truth was that he had not known he was drowning!

In terms of control, this whole marriage to Maddie was already going seriously off the rails. His goal had been to save Aida so that she could have what he had resigned himself to never having: true love. Was it the utter romance of the wedding that was making him feel the gaping wound of emptiness where love could not be?

Or was it what he had seen in Maddie's eyes right now? A chance. An opportunity to know love.

Impossible. Dancing with that particular dream could only get her seriously hurt. Nursing such fantasies couldn't be good for him, either!

What was the point of saving Aida, if he crushed another young woman's hopes and dreams and prospects in the process?

"What a mess I've made," Edward muttered out loud as he made his way to the safety of his bedroom on board the plane. Well, he could not undo what had been done. He could not take back the kisses they had shared—ones where he had actually felt as if the earth shifted under his feet.

He knew himself to be a strong man. But not strong enough to resist the invitation he had tasted on her lips, and seen in her eyes, and sensed in the soft pliability of her body underneath his when they had collapsed together on the bed just now.

He had to avoid her. In the morning, he had the plane return him to Havenhurst alone, and then sent it back to her.

And so began the most miserable period of the Prince's entire life. While he stayed away—eating in the palace dining room and making sure his business interests consumed his days—his suite underwent the most amazing metamorphosis.

When he stumbled in at night, too exhausted, thank God, to think of Maddie—her eyes, her lips, his longing for her conversation, or a hand of poker—he noticed portraits that had hung for hundreds of years had disappeared. He didn't want to know how she got them down, or what she did with them as staff were still banished from the suite.

Walls—some of them eighteen feet tall—were washed, filling his house with the clean scent of new beginnings. Then they were painted, heart-stoppingly tall ladders leaning about the place. One wall in the living room was painted a burnt orange that should have hurt the eyes, but somehow warmed the soul instead. Cheerful abstracts and art that showed things like little children in rowboats, cottages behind masses of flowers, puppies chewing on old boots, took their place.

Early, early in the morning, when he rose to avoid her, he noticed curtains had come down and light spilled in. He had paused to look at the changes, when her bedroom door squeaked open.

Her hair was a mess, and her pajamas were crumpled.

She looked adorable. And gorgeous. Somehow, impossibly, she looked sexy.

And so hopeful. As if maybe they could sit and have a coffee together. Talk. Yearning leaped in him.

"I hope you are not getting up on those ladders yourself," he told her curtly.

The sleepiness was gone in a second. She had lifted a rebellious eyebrow at him.

"I am ordering you to stay off those ladders."

She had stared at him for a moment, and then stuck out her tongue at him, flounced back into her room and slammed the door.

But underlying that show of feistiness, had there been sadness in her eyes? Despite the metamorphosis to his home, was he responsible for some new insecurity in her? He hated that. And didn't know what to do about it without getting in over his head.

Only his own room remained untouched. She never came in it, and as soon as he closed the door at night, instead of feeling safe, instead of feeling as if he had a sanctuary from her, he could feel the acute emptiness, the lack of her, somehow. Every day his bedroom seemed a little darker and a little danker and a little colder in comparison to all the places she had touched. Sometimes, it seemed to him, it was the kind of room a bitter old man would have: surrounded by his riches, his heart impoverished.

Combining with the smell of paint and cleanliness, in every room but his, was the underlying smell of good things cooking: the delicate aroma of scones, fresh-baked bread, cookies. He didn't know where she was finding the time for all this, or where all the goodies went, but they seemed to disappear as fast as she made them. When he pressed Lancaster, he found out she was baking for the whole regiment.

He also found out Maddie had taken to walking to town every day, taking the steep steps down the cliff, her shopping basket over her arm. She had accepted the security personnel, but refused to let her security detail carry her groceries. She greeted everyone she met. She stopped and exchanged pleasantries. She listened to problems. She hugged babies and old people.

She had, according to Lancaster, found a drop-in center for young people, and once a week she taught a group of young mothers how to make scones.

Of course, Ward ran into her by accident, though sometimes he wondered if she wasn't trying to catch him. He was curt rather than cordial. The invitation to come into the warmth she was creating never flagged in her eyes. He never quit resisting it with all his might, and the hurt in her eyes at his rejection always seemed brand-new.

Over time, she stopped trying so hard to engage him. She became more impersonal with him when they were together for official functions. She talked to him about the people she met. Sometimes she asked him to intercede in a problem that had been brought to her. She wanted him to look at putting a bakery in a vacant main street shop, so she could start a proper business and training program for her "girls."

He limited public engagements together, but there were several official engagements he could not avoid, and they attended as a couple.

He didn't make the mistake of touching her. He thought it would be perfect if they were the same kind of royal couple that his mother and father were.

It was at these public engagements that Prince Edward found out how much her little trips to town had been winning her favor.

People knew who she was. And they loved her with a

kind of simple devotion. Maddie, at these gatherings, performed as if she had been born to the role of princess. She was gracious, natural, good-humored and compassionate.

The fact that she was making such a good life for herself without him took away some of the guilt he was feeling that he had brought her into this.

And, if he was completely honest, made him jealous, too!

He thought he probably could have gone on this way indefinitely. Until one night he came home very late and heard the sound of quiet crying.

His head told him not to investigate.

But his heart refused to listen. He followed the sound through the darkened apartment and to Maddie's bedroom. The door was slightly ajar.

He went in, and stood for a moment, stunned by the transformation in the room. It was brightness itself, rich jewel tones on the bedding, on the new curtains that hung on the brightly painted walls. He wanted to stand here forever, breathing it—breathing her—in, as if he could never get enough.

But the sound of her muffled sobs drew him deeper into the room.

Where was she? And then he saw her. Lying on the bathroom floor. He thought his heart would stop beating at the fear he felt.

And then he raced to her.

CHAPTER SEVENTEEN

MADDIE FOUND HERSELF lifted off the floor. Ward sank down onto the edge of the tub with her cradled against his body. She felt the comforting heat of him, and drank in his scent. It was like homecoming and it made her cry harder.

"What have you done?" he asked. "I suppose you've fallen off one of your damned ladders?"

His voice was so harsh. But his touch was so tender. She turned her face into his chest and wept.

"What is it?" he insisted. "Are you hurt? Maddie, talk to me."

"Your mother invited me for tea," she finally choked out.

"If she's done something to you, I'll—"

"Done something to me? Oh no, it wasn't like that at all."

"What was it like then?"

"She served these awful things. She called them sausages, but they looked like pickles. They were even green."

"Blarneycockles," Ward said. "A local delicacy. But not for the uninitiated. Surely, you're not crying over blarneycockles, love?"

Love. She savored it. She let it wrap around her.

"Glenrich has been helping me with protocol. I knew I should just follow her lead. She took two and I took two. The smell was dreadful, but I couldn't refuse to eat what she was eating. So, I took a bite. Nowhere in the protocol book does it tell you what to do if you feel a desire to heave while lunching with the Queen."

"Over a blarneycockle? They're not that bad!"

"They are! I didn't know what to do, and then one of the horrid dogs started creating a ruckus. I put one down my skirt, and pretended to nibble away on the other and then the horrid dog attacked the little one, and while your mother was distracted by that, I disposed of the other one. The second blarneycockle."

"Down your skirt?"

"Please don't laugh. It's not a laughing matter."

"I'm sorry."

"I didn't know what to do with them. I wanted to just put them in the garbage, but I thought what if somebody notices and reports to the Queen I didn't eat them?"

"It's hardly a hanging offense, even in Havenhurst."

"I felt as if we were getting along famously."

"You and my mother?" he said incredulously.

"I understand her," she said softly. "I know I haven't been here long, but I understand her loneliness. Everyone is eager to please. Everyone does whatever you ask them to do. But nobody is honest with you. No one would tell you if you had spinach on your teeth. No one feels they can be your friend. It's kind of this awful awe and fear mixed, and you can't overcome it, no matter what you do."

"You're crying because you're lonely?" he asked, stricken.

"I guess partly. Partly because of something else your mother said."

"What?" What had his mother said?

"I asked your mother about the kind of little boy you were—"

"And she knew?" he asked, amazed.

"Of course, she knew. She talked about the time you

fell off your pony, and you were crying, and your father told you to man up, and you did. And then later they found out your arm was broken. She teared up, telling that story."

"My mother? Teared up?"

"Yes. And so did I."

He felt something clog his own throat at the thought of these two women feeling such compassion for him.

"It wasn't that big a deal," he said stiffly, staving off what the compassion in her eyes was making him feel.

She looked at him long and hard, but she must have learned her lesson about trying to connect with him, because she brushed at her tearstained face and turned her attention back to the toilet.

"I've plugged the toilet with the blasted blarneycockles, and I can't get it apart."

"You're trying to get the toilet apart?" he asked with horror.

"Well, I can't call anyone. I'd be the laughingstock of the whole palace, wouldn't I? And then word would get back to your mother, and she would think I was sneaky and deceitful, and maybe I am."

"You are not!"

"Look at our marriage, Ward," she said softly.

Apparently he would rather look at blarneycockles plugging the toilet, than at their marriage, because he set her down firmly and went and flipped open the lid.

"I don't see anything," he said.

"That's because they're caught in the trap."

"The what?"

"The trap, the curve where the pipe bends around."

"Oh."

"Do you see why I'm lonely, Ward?" she asked him softly. "I'm a logger's daughter who comes from a place where we had to be self-sufficient and self-reliant. The only people in this castle who are like that won't talk to me, at least not as a friend."

"I can fix this," he said, with determination, and when he lifted his eyes and looked at her, she saw something new in them.

And she saw he was not talking about just the toilet.

"Why don't we fix it together?" she asked. And she wasn't talking about the toilet, either.

But that was where they started, prying the rusty bolts off the bowl and lifting it off the seal and screaming with laughter as water went everywhere.

With as much bravery as she had ever seen in a man, he donned the rubber gloves and stuck his hand in there, and came up with first one and then the other blarney-cockle.

"Damn slippery," he said as one slid through his hand. She chased it across the bathroom floor, but then couldn't bring herself to touch it. He picked it up and wagged his eyebrows fiendishly at her, thrusting the disgusting blarneycockle toward her.

She took off running, and shrieking with laughter, they chased each other through every room of that apartment until both of them were breathless with exertion.

Still laughing, they wrapped the horrid green sausages in newspapers, and then in plastic bags, and then put them in a box.

They cleaned up all the water and washed to the elbow at least a dozen times, when he finally admitted he still didn't feel clean.

"Me, either."

"I know a secret place," he said.

And she did, too. And she knew, finally, they were heading straight toward it, the secret guarded fortress of Prince Edward's heart.

And if they got there by way of the palace garbage dumpster, muffling their laughter in pitch blackness as they got rid of the blarneycockle box, so be it.

Ward shouldered a pack he had brought. The palace grounds were extremely dark, but he knew his way perfectly. As they circled around the dark ramparts of the castle, Maddie felt as if they were explorers embarking on a great adventure. They came to a place in the wall where there was a large, prickly hawthorne.

"Careful," he said, as he shoved it aside and protected her from the worst of the prickles. Behind the thick shrub was a hole in the wall. He paused and fished around in the pack until he found a flashlight.

He lit it and she saw a tunnel stretched before them until it dipped suddenly, steeply out of sight.

With her hand in his, ducking in places because the tunnel was so narrow, they went where it led. She could smell it before they arrived. It felt like homecoming.

"Hot springs!"

"Underground. I found them when I was a boy. I don't think anyone else knows about them. When I was a child, it felt so lovely to have a secret. I would tell my nanny I was reading in my room, and then I would slip out the window. And, for a few hours I would be free."

She felt the deep honor of his sharing this place with her.

The tunnel gave way to a cave, the ceiling dripping with stalactites. The cave was open to a sheltered bay of the sea, and stars winked through an opening in the cave ceiling. Small waterfalls cascaded down the sides of the cliff and into a deeply turquoise pool with steam rising off the water.

"Here we are," she said huskily, "back at hot pools. It's like a full circle, isn't it?"

"It's a chance to start again," he said quietly. He opened the pack and pulled two thick towels from it. He turned off the flashlight. She heard his clothes whisper to the floor. Surely he had something on? Surely he had brought suits?

"No clothes allowed," he told her, from the darkness of the pool. "For me, it was part of being free. No rules, at all. No one watching."

"But you're watching!" she whispered.

"I can't even see my hand in front of my face."

That was true. The darkness inside the cave was the pitch-black variety. She hesitated, but only for a second. And then she let her clothes fall in a puddle at her feet. Wearing only her gold chain, and the nugget that dangled from it, Maddie stepped toward the water, feeling her way along the slippery floor with her toe. There it was. She stepped in, gingerly, and felt the water close on her naked skin.

It was truly the most sensual thing she had ever felt. Until Ward reached for her in the darkness, until his hand found hers. Her eyes adjusted, slowly, to the darkness, but the water cloaked both of them. Save for his face, the drops of water on his lashes, the line of his nose, the fullness of his lower lip, the cleft of his chin, illuminated by starlight.

She leaned toward him, but he let her go, gave a gentle teasing splash and moved away from her. They played tag in the darkness, just as they had when they first met. They played tag and laughed and discovered the joy of each other. Because the water hid them, she didn't feel shy.

But then, unexpectedly, Ward hefted himself from the pool and raced for the sea. For a moment she was totally hypnotized by his perfect form, by the poetry of the faint starlight cascading off his wet body, by his sureness and his freedom. He threw himself into the cold water and his shout of pure exhilaration echoed through the cave.

Elation such as she had never felt shivered along her spine.

This magnificent man was her husband.

Maddie stood for a moment, knowing he was watching her, and then went into the sea behind him. The cold water embraced her heated flesh.

And then Ward was beside her, and his hands were in the wet tangle of her hair, and his body was hot and smooth against hers, taking the chill from the water.

His lips claimed hers. In them was everything that love was: power and freedom and something completely untamable, unconquerable, the force that was life itself.

Her lips opened to the command of his, and her heart opened to his need.

She became his wife, and she knew, gladly, with a tremulous song in her heart, that her life would never be the same again.

Losing control, Ward discovered, was like letting a dragon out of a box. It would not go back in again. It did not obey orders. It scorned efforts to dominate it.

The fire in him was a dragon that had tasted something foreign and forbidden and could now not get enough.

Ward fell in love with his wife. He fell in love with the secrets of her body and the intricacies of her mind. He fell in love with her laughter. And the way she looked sitting with her feet up on the sofa reading a book.

He fell in love with her fearlessness as he taught her to dive. He fell in love with her endless baking. He fell in love with her delight as he revealed to her all the secrets of his island—the patches of wild lupines that grew by the hot springs, and the secret paths and groves that led to old ruins, and churches and crumbling castles. To Lancaster's rather tolerant dismay they became experts at giving him the slip.

He fell in love with her quiet as he revealed all his own secrets and fears.

He fell in love with her as he watched her blossom into a true princess. She started her bakery with her girls.

His mother adored her. Even his father seemed amazed by this force of love and light that had been brought to their island.

In her, in Maddie, in his beautiful wife, he had found the place his heart had always longed for, the place he wanted so badly he feared it.

Not that he planned to jinx it by saying it out loud!

CHAPTER EIGHTEEN

MADDIE WOKE WITH a start. It was midafternoon. Why was she so tired all the time? Her stomach rolled. Not a blarneycockle in sight. In fact, she'd had a cheese sandwich for lunch. Her stomach rolled again, and she raced for the bathroom.

The flu, she thought after, as she wiped her mouth. She caught a glimpse of her reflection in the mirror above the sink.

She stared at herself. Her hair had grown quite a bit, wild curls softening into waves that framed her face. Gone were the worry lines that had looked back at her such a short time ago. Her face looked more than relaxed—it looked radiant.

"You don't look like a woman with the flu," she told herself.

And then the truth hit her.

It was not possible. They had only been unprotected that once, the first time they had gone to the secret underground pools. After that, Ward was always prepared.

And it was a good thing, too, because they seemed intent on exploring every secret of each other in every secluded enclave and hot spring on the whole island. They had become experts at ditching Lancaster, though he didn't seem to mind.

Maddie walked out of her bathroom in a daze and sank down on her bed. She counted on her fingers. And then counted again.

A baby.

The joy that rose in her was quickly overtaken by doubt. She was no more prepared to have a baby now than she had been when she had experienced that pregnancy scare in her past.

The situation even had similarities! She was besotted, and he was... What?

Not certain of his feelings, obviously, since he had never spoken of them. Maybe, just like that boy from long ago, he had taken what was offered but thought there were no strings attached. Their marriage was not supposed to be a real one.

For all the intimacy they enjoyed, Ward had never once said he wanted to change the terms of their agreement.

In fact, thinking back on it, just like that other boy, he had never once said he loved her. Didn't the fact he had always, always been prepared after that first time, speak volumes to the complication to their relationship that he did not want?

Oh, he would do the honorable thing! Of course he would. How horrible to have the man you loved so madly, whose baby you were almost certain you carried, do his duty by you.

To be the one who trapped him, exactly as he had been trapped by circumstances his entire life.

Maddie felt she was not a person who had trouble making decisions. Look how quickly she had decided to become Ward's wife!

And yet, suddenly, she did not know what to do. She was acutely aware she had no one, aside from Ward, to take into her confidence. His mother had warmed to her, but in this circumstance, how could she trust her?

Or him for that matter.

Lancaster adored her, but his first loyalty was not to her.

Carrying the royal baby was probably a very serious matter, indeed.

They would think the baby belonged to them. Her child was the heir to the island kingdom of Havenhurst.

Maddie felt such a rush of fierce protectiveness it nearly knocked her over. She needed some space. She had to figure out, and quickly—if the count she had just done on her fingers was correct—what to do. She had to figure out what to do, not just for herself, but for the ultimate good of the child.

You didn't just leave Havenhurst. There was one flight out once a week. And there were three boats every week. If she said she had to leave, questions would be asked. Though she had become accustomed to it, Maddie was not allowed to travel anywhere by herself. A guard always followed discreetly. She did not think that love of her scones would be enough for any one of them to overcome their sense of duty and smuggle her out of the country.

Duty, she thought angrily.

But she had no time to indulge her thoughts. Only action counted now. If she used a phone in the palace, they would trace it when she was missing. They would know who she had called.

Grabbing her cloak, aware as never before of the guard that dogged her, she walked quickly to town.

The bakery was bustling. The girls smiled and nodded at her, but it was very crowded. Hardly anybody noticed her slip into the back room and take the phone off its hook. She was trembling so badly it took her three times to remember how to dial an international number, even though she had been checking in with Kettle and Sophie regularly.

Thankfully, despite the differences in time, Kettle answered. He'd obviously been sleeping, but came awake with that alertness that anyone who had served active duty never quite lost.

"I need your help," she said. "Kettle, I'm in trouble."

Kettle did not say he had told her so. Every time she had talked to him since her hasty marriage to the Prince, he was no closer to forgiving her for bailing him out, and for saving the Black Kettle. In fact he was furious about it.

But this was the thing about family—about the families you were born to and the ones that you chose—the love was always there.

And that was all she heard in his gruff voice. The love.

"Tell me what you need."

She did. It seemed she was making an impossible request.

But he only said, "You did the right thing to call. I'll be there for you as quickly as I can."

She could not cry in front of her girls.

Ward had been away for three days. Maddie had not come with him on this trip, saying something was going on at the bakery that needed her.

He couldn't believe how much he missed her. He went into their suite, so eager to see her, to hold her, to talk to her, that it felt as if he was vibrating at his core.

"Maddie?" he called.

There was something about the emptiness, about the way that his voice echoed back to him that made the hair stand up on the back of his neck.

Ridiculous. She would just be at the bakery, or visiting with his mother, or perhaps delivering scones to the besotted members of the palace guard. Perhaps, she'd been invited, at the last moment, to hand out certificates at the kindergarten graduation ceremonies or trophies at the Senior's Centre Annual Lawn Bowling Tournament.

Lancaster would know where she was.

Then he saw the envelope, a white square sitting on the kitchen table. He felt his heart sink to the bottom of his toes. He picked it up with trembling hands and a shadow of premonition.

He opened it and scanned the words.

Need time. Please understand. Don't try to find me.

How was that possible? He thought back over the last few days he had spent with her. Delightful. With the underlying intensity of the freed dragon.

He wanted to believe his father had done something. Or his mother. But he knew it wasn't that. He knew it was him. Somehow he had disappointed. Hurt her. Been insensitive. She had seen what he came from—the coldness between people, the remoteness, the lack of connection— and she had decided, probably wisely, to extricate herself.

And he wondered how could he have forgotten the dragon's flames destroyed everything in their path?

But how could she have done it? How was it no one had noticed she was missing? And was she safe? She was a public figure now. Her face was known around the world. What if someone harmed her?

He called Lancaster. "Maddie is missing."

"Missing? I don't understand."

He didn't want to share his greatest failure with anyone, but her safety might be compromised. Contemplating that made Ward feel physically ill. If something happened to her, it was on him.

Within minutes Lancaster was there with a report. "She left a note on a bag of scones for her security this morning.

She said she was staying home and wouldn't go for her walk. There's no way she got off the island. There's one flight and three sailings. None of them last night. We'll watch the ones today. We'll search the island. We'll find her. I promise."

And Lancaster kept his promise.

But it was three days later, and the big man had obviously not slept or eaten. Ward had barely slept or eaten, either. So far, the fact the Princess was missing was only known by those who needed to know.

"She's not on Havenhurst," Lancaster said.

"What? How?"

"I don't have the details, yet. I pried it out of Sophie."

"Where is Maddie?"

"I don't have her exact location. Sophie didn't know that. But I know who does know."

"Kettle," he said quietly. "Let's go."

"The jet is already waiting. Sir, he's not the kind of man you're going to be able to get it out of."

Ward considered that. He knew it was true: no threat would work. Probably torture would not even work.

But there was something that might.

The truth.

CHAPTER NINETEEN

MADDIE WALKED THE long sandy shore of Cannon Beach, hugging herself against the nippy wind coming off the ocean. Somehow, the last few days seemed more of a dream than marrying Prince Edward had seemed.

Kettle had found a crew of hardened old Navy SEALs like himself. They whisked her away from Havenhurst with an ease that was matched only by their secrecy. Then, Kettle had a friend with this little cottage in Cannon Beach. She was there for now, blending in with all the tourists, in a ball cap pulled over a face mostly hidden by large sunglasses. She had taken to wearing red lipstick, which made her nearly unrecognizable to herself.

Maddie felt the oddest combination of grief and elation. She missed Ward with a physical ache. And yet the baby felt real already, filling her with a quiet sense of calm and determination. She was not bringing a baby into the world with a father who did not want it.

A long time ago, she had realized you could not wait for a man to rescue you. Not even a prince. Here was the thing: you had to rescue yourself.

And so even though she was in the worst predicament of her life—having left a man she loved with all her heart, practically hiding because of her unwanted fame, with no resources besides the love of those closest to her—she felt certain that she could do this.

She could make a safe haven and a safe life for her baby. She felt differently than she had when she'd had her previous pregnancy scare. So differently. There was no panic at all, but rather a deep sense of all being well for her and for her child. And it wasn't just that she was older. Even though her love with Ward had not been reciprocated, something about loving him had made her braver, not afraid to love and to love fiercely.

This was a gift she would give to her baby.

She saw a man coming toward her and started.

No, it could not be him. It couldn't be. And yet her heart raced as if it was, and as he drew closer, there was no doubt. For a panicky moment she wanted to run. He would see in her face her love for him, her need.

But he had probably only come because he had figured it out. He had figured out she carried the royal baby.

He couldn't make her go back against her will.

He came closer and she was taken aback. Ward looked glorious, and yet there were dark circles under his eyes, and a thinness to his face he had not had before. Finally, he drew in front of her and thrust his hands deep in his pockets. He scanned her face and then looked away to where puffins screeched off Haystack Rock.

His face looked so tormented. She wanted to touch it. But she followed his lead and put her hands in the pockets of the hooded jacket she was wearing.

"Ward," she said.

"Maddie."

"How did you find me?"

"Kettle told me."

"Kettle would never tell you."

"Not if I tortured him, I'm sure. Or threatened him. The truth was a different matter."

"The truth?" she whispered.

"Maddie, why? Why did you leave?"

"I told you in the note. I needed some time to think."

"Just so suddenly?" he asked. "I thought we were doing so well. Given the circumstances."

"The circumstances," she said. "A fake marriage, that we were both treating as if it was real."

"Maddie, I'm so sorry."

"Sorry?"

"I know it's me. I know we've had great fun, but I don't blame you for coming to your senses. I know you saw what I came from, and I know the deep love you came from, and you realized it was unworkable. That I can never be the man you want. And deserve. I'm sorry I put you through all of this. Of course, you are free to leave. I'll ask for an annulment right away. But I hope you will accept security—personal and financial—for as long as it takes for it all to fade away."

An annulment, she thought, dully. And, of course, his ever-present sense of honor. He would look after her, even though it had not worked out.

But then she looked at the torment on his face and let his words sink in.

He didn't think he was good enough? He didn't think he could give her what she deserved? That's why he was going to set her free?

He didn't know about the baby. He didn't have a clue.

"Are you here because you are trying to do what is best for me?" she breathed.

The question seemed to take him by surprise.

"Of course."

"Look, this seems strange to me. Are you, the Prince, telling me, a common girl, you are somehow unworthy of me?"

"I think you figured that out. You need a man who knows how to love you in the way you deserve to be loved. I think you realized that's not me."

"You think you don't know how to love?" Maddie asked, incredulous.

"How could I know that?" he growled, his pain raw in his voice.

"Ward, you don't think putting Aida's needs ahead of your own was a form of love?"

He tilted his head at her. "A form, I suppose."

"And what about the relationship between you and Lancaster? You don't think that's a form of love? He's like your brother!"

"Well, maybe—"

"And what about the way you treat your niece, Anne? You're playful with her, and yet it is so obvious you would lay down your life to protect her if need be."

"Of course, I would."

"That's love. How do you feel right now, this instant, standing here, telling me you'll let me go?"

"Broken," he said, his voice low and strained. "It feels as if letting you go is tearing the heart out of me."

"Ward," she asked softly, "don't you think that's love? Putting what you think are another person's needs ahead of your own? How did you find me?"

"Kettle."

"Do you think Kettle would have sent you here, if he didn't see the truth in you?"

He ducked his head. "Why make this harder? It's obvious I have feelings for you. I've decided I'm not the best person for you."

She reached up and touched his face, cupped the side of it, his chin in her palm.

"Say it," she said.

"Oh, Maddie, always telling me what to do. The only

person who orders the Prince around. But must you hear this? Must you have my heart at your feet?"

"Yes," she said.

"All right." He refused to look at her. "I love you. I love everything about you. I would give up my whole kingdom for one more day of chasing you through the hot springs. For one more hand of poker. For one more kiss. For one more opportunity to hold you.

"I've never felt this way before. I did not know it was possible to feel this way.

"And for that, I thank you. That I have been allowed the great privilege of knowing love, however briefly. It has made me a better man."

Her eyes filmed with tears and they fell.

He lifted his hand and traced the path of one down her cheek. "See? Now, I've made you cry. I'm inept at this business. I'm sorry. I'll go. I don't know why I came. I just had to see you one more time, to look at your face…"

"Ward, be quiet. Look at me."

And then he did look at her face. He looked at it long and hard, like a man who had had a drink from a cool pool of water, and knew he would never drink from it again.

But as he looked at her, something in his own expression changed. He saw it. He saw her love for him shining out of her.

"You don't have a clue, do you?" she asked him softly.

"I'm afraid—"

"Ward, I didn't leave because I don't love you. I left because I did."

"I'm not following. At all."

"You really don't know?"

He shook his head, baffled, and yet hope had risen in his eyes.

"I'm pregnant, Ward. I'm going to have our baby."

"What?"

He fell on his knees before her. He gently opened her jacket and ran his hands over the smoothness of her belly. He kissed it.

"I thought—" She was crying hard now. "I thought when you found out, you would feel an obligation to make our marriage real. I couldn't have that. I couldn't be married to you without love. Without knowing the child would be loved."

He rose to his feet and gathered her hard against him.

"How could you not know I loved you?"

"I don't know," she said, staring up at him from within the circle of his arms. "I don't know why the words seemed so important, when it is so clear to me right now that you were telling me in so many different ways all the time. I think being pregnant frightened me."

He looked stricken that anything he had done—or not done—had frightened her.

"I didn't know how to say those words," Ward admitted. "But I know how, now, and I will never stop saying them. I will never stop loving you. Or our baby. I will love you both until the end of time and beyond. This is my vow to you."

She felt it. She felt the truth, not just of his words, but the truth of his heart, to the bottom of her soul. She felt the truth of it, of the power of love.

And at last she was home.

EPILOGUE

PRINCE EDWARD ALEXANDER THE FOURTH stood with a baby in his arms and his heart in his throat.

He looked way up, to the rock outcropping above the top pool of Honeymoon Hot Springs.

Maddie stood there, poised, arms straight out in front of her, on the tips of her toes.

He wanted to shout at her not to, but she was still the only person in his world who did not listen to him.

She gathered herself, and Ward saw what all the people of Havenhurst saw in their beloved Princess: she was of the earth.

But when she launched and soared upward, he saw what he alone was allowed to see.

She was not just of the earth. She was also of the sky.

She was a bird who had found its wings. She spread her arms wide, embracing the air and the sky, and Ward saw her strength and her grace and her confidence in herself. He saw her bravery and her tenacity. And he saw that she did not need him.

Which made the fact that she chose him all the more remarkable.

Maddie had come into herself even more since the baby was born. One of those women who blossomed under love.

His love. His imperfect, stumbling along, learning new and magnificent things every day kind of love.

As he watched, she jackknifed and did a perfect, almost-splashless entry into the water of the pool. A few seconds later she surfaced, laughing, shaking droplets of water from her hair.

This was the first time they had been back in Mountain Bend since the mineral water bottling plant had opened here, after Havenhurst had shared its technology and marketing with the mountain village. Already the town was prospering from the work generated by that pant. Already the sales of that healing mineral water were through the roof.

But it didn't hurt that a sign hung at the entrance of the town saying it was the birthplace of Madeline, Princess of Havenhurst. People were intrigued. They came to see, out of curiosity, and stayed because there was something here that had been lost.

The town represented the purity, the innocence, the wholesomeness of times past. And because it still had those rare things, and had them in abundance, Mountain Bend was thriving—little cottages lovingly restored, shops busy, people happy.

"Great dive," he said.

Maddie lifted herself out of the water. She was wearing a two-piece, but the thrill he felt was even deeper than the first time he had seen her here, and it had nothing to do with her choice of bathing attire.

"Your turn," she said, holding out her arms for the chubby, gurgling baby. He had been named Ryan. Prince Ryan Lancaster the First. It was not a historical royal name, but honored both Maddie's father and the man who had been so much more than a protector, more like a brother to Ward. It was rare, however, for Maddie to call Ryan either of his given names. To the delight of the people of Havenhurst, who loved her so much, she mostly called the baby Prince Chunky Monkey.

Ward left her and scrambled up the rocks until he stood

high above his wife and his baby. He threw open his arms to the sky, but somehow he did not jump.

No, he stood there, in gratitude and in wonder.

A long time ago, that night that had changed everything, that night when he had asked Maddie to be his wife, Ward had not really ever considered the nature of miracles.

But now he did.

He had been a prince, one of the richest, most successful, most admired men in the world. And yet he had been impoverished.

It was love that made him who he was.

It was love that had crowned him King.

He bounced on his toes. Once. Twice. He was aware, not of the wealth of being a prince—he had found out you could be intensely poor, while the whole world admired your outward signs of riches—but of the wealth of being alive.

He tingled with recognition of the utter abundance of this moment, birdsong, the scent of the forest beyond him and the scent of the ponds beneath him. Of Maddie, watching, that wiggly baby held firmly in her arms, her upturned face alight.

It was love that made you alive.

On three, Prince Edward Alexander launched off the rock, then tucked into himself and somersaulted through the air, opened into a twist, and then cleanly cut into the calmness of the waiting water.

He surfaced, laughing joyously, aware he was still showing off for his Princess. And he hoped that would never end.

* * * * *

LET'S TALK
Romance

For exclusive extracts, competitions
and special offers, find us online:

f facebook.com/millsandboon

⊙ @millsandboonuk

🐦 @millsandboon

Or get in touch on 0844 844 1351*

For all the latest titles coming soon,
visit millsandboon.co.uk/nextmonth